In The Beginning
A novel by
Daizal.R.Samad

Introduced by Ashwannie Harripersaud

BLUEROSE PUBLISHERS
India | U.K.

Copyright © Daizal R. Samad 2024

All rights reserved by author. No part of this publication may be reproduced, stored in a retrieval system or transmitted in any form or by any means, electronic, mechanical, photocopying, recording or otherwise, without the prior permission of the author. Although every precaution has been taken to verify the accuracy of the information contained herein, the publisher assume no responsibility for any errors or omissions. No liability is assumed for damages that may result from the use of information contained within.

BlueRose Publishers takes no responsibility for any damages, losses, or liabilities that may arise from the use or misuse of the information, products, or services provided in this publication.

For permissions requests or inquiries regarding this publication, please contact:

BLUEROSE PUBLISHERS
www.BlueRoseONE.com
info@bluerosepublishers.com
+91 8882 898 898
+4407342408967

ISBN: 978-93-6452-898-6

Cover design: Tahira
Typesetting: Tanya Raj Upadhyay

First Edition: August 2024

INTRODUCTION

On the surface, this novel is a fictional account of the birth and genesis of what was to become one of the world's most influential systems of belief. This system of belief was spread through violent colonization that had to be endured for about six hundred years. In the process, the world was reshaped, and the adherents are now to be counted in billions. As it spread through the continents over the centuries the system of belief became progressively less monolithic. Tribal differences and cultural accommodations to indigenous cultures were two significant causes of divisions, splinters, variations, and adjustments. Despite these facts, there is much extant sermonizing about the "sameness" of the religion. The sermonizing is constant and ubiquitous.

The violent conquest and forced conversion of large swaths of Africa and India, among other places, changed those places irredeemably and irreversibly. That seems obvious. Again, though, there is much sermonizing that it is against the rules—the English word used is "unholy"—to convert anyone forcibly. The spread became greater when converts themselves began converting others. What is not so obvious and goes unadmitted is that the forms the system of belief took also depended on the culture it absorbed and that absorbed it. The sometimes-subtle mutations in religious practice cover a wide range of behaviors—from outward forms of worship to the treatment of women, to food, to dress. But to point out any of this—especially to the converted or those converted by converts—would elicit outrage since it goes up against the insistence of "sameness". As they see it, when these differences are identified or pointed out, it is an accusation of inauthenticity. . Any kind of critical examination, however, demonstrates that religious beliefs have always generated greater fervency than cultural attachments (or logic, for that matter).

On the other hand, differences in clothes, climate, eating habits, language, and so on, are easily ignored or explained away. That denial takes the form of exact, unthinking imitation and repetition. For instance, desert garb, designed toprotect from harsh desert conditions long before any religions began, is now worn in places with year-round pleasant weather. The manner of dress for females—full covering in drab colors—serves as a means of announcing one's religious affiliation. It announces the firmness of one's devotion to the system of belief and pronounces a conspicuous difference from the rest of society. It may also announce obedience to the male of the household who insists on the female following the rules dictating female covering, ostensibly done to protect female modesty while avoiding the temptation that women are said to present to males.

At the same time, Western laws, imposed by European colonizers, are followed because there are legal consequences for breaking those laws. A man may have only one wife and vice versa by law, or else charges of bigamy can be brought by the state. There are no such inhibitors in desert cultures. Outside of these cultures, the treatment of women has had to be adjusted to follow Western laws. For instance, spousal abuse can result in imprisonment and women are permitted to drive. Of course, men also wear long beards and *disdashas* (long robes) as overt signals of religious affiliation, but this now also seems to be a superficial signal of pride, and easy rebellion. There are no legal consequences since in Western cultures people are free to dress however they wish.

In countries that have come under the yoke of European colonization, the converted even proclaim their faith and degree of devotion by writing on vehicles, as if such overt declarations are assurances of depth or sincerity of faith. They may intend to signal that, but it is just as likely that they may be caveats of insecurity, a sense of not quite being the "real thing". To be fair, these declarations of faith on windscreens and other places on vehicles cut across all the major faiths in the Commonwealth: Christianity, Hinduism, and Islam. Vehicles are frequently proclaimed as "GIFTS" from one deity or another.

Language is yet another bone of contention in converted nations that have a language or languages of their own. The faith in question here explicitly forbids translation (and therefor interpretation) to other languages. Prayers are offered up in the language of the people who are of the place where the system of belief originated. Call to prayers, greetings, and other utterances like "God is great", "praise be to God", and "with the will of God" are uttered in the original language. Yet, the vast majority of adherents worldwide simply mouth that original language with only a vague understanding of what they are saying in prayer. Specialized schools are run with the exclusive intention of memorizing the holy book and its ancillaries. Memorizing without understanding is the antithesis of education.

Again, this is not at all unique. Hindus pray in Sanskrit but understand little or nothing about the language. And how many Christians (or professed Christians) understand the language of the King James Bible? The answer comes easily when we listen to them read a passage from that book. They almost invariably mangle the language. The evidence of scant knowledge of the Bible is perpetually on display by "megapastors" preaching the "prosperity gospel". They "speak in tongues" and enthralltheir millions of followers by screaming into microphones, clowning, jumping up and down, demanding money in exchange for more money, performing "miracles", and overtly involving themselves in right-wing politics. Little or nothing to do with the good works of the Christ or the scriptures, but everything to do with coin and ragged politics.

The more recent versions of the Christian Bible amount to rather poor attempts in modernizing the language of Jacobian England but succeeding merely in diluting the poetry of Shakespeare and the English Renaissance. For instance, the line in Psalm 23 which reads "He [God] maketh me to lie beside green pastures" becomes "He makes me lie beside green pastures". The entire meaning and tone changes: in the first, God has made us to enjoy the pleasures of the lushness and plenty of the earth"; in the second, God is commanding us to go and lie besides green pastures. The gap between language and understanding is wide indeed.

For both systems of belief that began in the Middle East, the languages in which they are conveyed are foreign to most of today's practitioners of those faiths. Christianity began with Hebrew and Aramaic followed by translations into various languages: Greek, Latin, English, and so on. There is no insistence on "holy language". There is also the intellectual recognition in thinking adherents that English has many variations: Australian English, Irish English, Scottish English, Malaysian English, West Indian English, Indian English, American English, to name a few, can be quite distinct. This is precisely why it is silly to speak of "Standard English" rather than "formal English".

INTRODUCTION

In very similar ways, there are dramatic variations in Arabic: The Arabic spoken in Morocco, Tunisia, Algeria, Saudi Arabia, Egypt, etc. can also be quite distinct. Unlike their Christian counterparts, however, the converted nations insist on the "holy language" argument. Translations are forbidden, yet most of the faithful outside of the Middle East depend on translations to grasp what meaning they can. We also hear the uncompromising claim that the holy book is the greatest poetry. But we cannot even read the language.

Discerning readers of Samad's **In the Beginning** will recognize the deliberate unevenness of language. When the characters try to elevate the importance of what is being said or when they are imitating a historical moment of importance, the language becomes almost poetic. In scenes of sordid violence, the language is flat, ordinary, prosaic. As in life, language becomes a measurement of the moral worth of the character. In Samad's In The Beginning, Kay's language is gentle and lofty because she is someone of moral worth; it is ameliorative without being obsequious.

The two major monotheistic religions—Christianity and Islam—had their beginnings in the arid Middle East. In one, the values and examples set in the beginnings seem to have been largely lost, especially in the so-called evangelical versions of the religion in the United States. In the other, today, in converted lands where water is plentiful and lands are lush, the manner of cleansing is slavishly identical to the customary habit of ordinary cleansing in places where water was a luxury almost two thousand years ago. With expansion and the passage of time and despite dramatic changes in geographical circumstances, the manner of pre-prayer cleansing has hardened into being a ritual as mandatory as the prayers themselves. There is no questioning, no thought involved, and there is also a lack of realization that this method of cleansing is grounded in two imperatives: firstly, water was scarce so a full bath or a shower was not possible. Secondly, in the lush lands consisting of hundreds of millions of converted peoples, there is no desert sand lodged in ears, mouth, nostrils, between toes and fingers, hair, and neck which was the case earlier. The pre-prayer cleansing that was a hygienic necessity in the desert has now mutated into a mandatory act of religious compulsion rather than a simple act of hygiene. This cleansing ritual (*wudun*) is clearly evident, in our times in 2024, when there is plumbing in the rapidly developed Middle East where Americans discovered oil in about 1926.

In countries that have declared themselves Islamic States—like Pakistan, Iran, Malaysia, and Indonesia—the adherents to ancient cultural habits born of either necessity or pre-Islamic traditions in the desert countries are now made to carry the burden of fierce devotion. To think and question is almost forbidden since they stand in opposition to submission. The longing is for a "pure" time, even as the craving is for the luxuries of modernity—electricity, ready potable water, expensive cars, high-rise buildings, technology, etc. One supposes that the amount of wealth oil brings in, allows for a kind of spiritual looking back while simultaneously looking forward to material benefits. Many of the converted nations have no such wealth at their disposal that would accommodate this paradox.

In the past two thousand years, the world has changed in ways we could not have imagined. There have been dazzling developments in economies, technologies, mechanics, infrastructure, communication, medicine, and so on. We have more knowledge at our fingertips now than at any other time in human history. We have found new ways to cure sicknesses; we have also found new ways to murder each other on a grand scale. In spite of this, humanity has remained largely unchanged, unevolved. We are still prone to being violent, treacherous, greedy, lustful, and murderous. With all the information available so easily, we remain padlocked in our solitudes, ignorant, arrogant, self-righteous, snarling at any stranger at our gate. We have unprecedented means of communicating with each other, but ironically we are the most isolated or lonely than ever before.

One of the major causes of our respective solitudes is our respective belief systems, and Christianity and Islam are two of the most insidious tools we use to keep ourselves firmly padlocked within our solitudes. Our self-isolation and tribalism make us susceptible to every political and religious charlatan with a microphone and a soap box. We babble endlessly about "critical thinking", "democracy", "communism", "wokeism", but are blissfully ignorant of the meanings of these and many more oft-used terms. Words have become bereft of meaning and depth, and an oath is just an utterance that evaporates once spoken out loud. Strangely, ethnic and cultural purity is much sought after and is only to be found in beginnings, origins. This yearning for the "pure times" stops the process of thinking, inhibits imagination and cripples learning. Anything that does not fit neatly into our vision of "purity" and the "pure times" is to be denied, rejected, reviled killed.

It is significant that no single religion has ever succeeded (or maybe even tried) to stop a war, but they are frequently used to stoke fear and start and sustain killing. The foundation always seems to be that our religion is superior; therefore, the adherents to our religion are superior. Simultaneously, your religion is inferior therefore you are inferior. Add the catalyst of racial superiority/ inferiority with politics, and we have perpetual killing. In the frenzy of bloodlust, we extinguish whatever good may be found in systems of religious belief. We have grown more and more certain in the correctness and superiority of our way of life and our way of worship; consequently we see all other ways as malevolent, hostile, deadly. And there is always fecund ground for greed. The two most destructive forms of colonization are built upon this certainty that one is right and righteous and superior; the other is false, evil, and inferior.

European colonization sprung from this idea of inferiority and superiority. The former must be "civilized and Christianized", brought out of their primitive ways. A great deal has been written on this, of course. In terms of novels, Joseph Conrad's <u>Heart of Darkness</u> shows the brutality and brutishness involved in the implementation of this idea. And yet, the faith had its beginnings in a man who preached peace, love, and the embrace of compassion.

Arab colonization also sprang from this idea of superiority and inferiority, but the aims were women and money rather than civilize and Christianize. This lasted 600 years, almost one hundred years longer than the other. Not much has been written about this, relatively speaking. Samad's **In the Beginning** compels us to ask this question: If the life and deeds of a truly good man could be so cruelly twisted as it has been, what grotesquerie would we have if there is a system of faith that had its beginnings in a man who was malevolent ?

Every system of belief has its own, often-unexamined substructure. Christianity is erected upon examples, set by the life and deeds of the Christ. These examples demonstrate how we may live with ourselves as individuals and in harmony with others. Unfortunately, we see the betrayal of these examples on a daily basis, but the same people involved in betrayal and self-betrayal profess their adherence to the religion with loud ferocity. Taoism is built upon the sublime philosophies of Lao Tze and Confucious. It encourages us to be more introspective and less violent. Hinduism is based on stories (or narratives) that draw no hard conclusions for us but leave us to draw our own inferences and chart our own moral paths. Those narratives have most often been reduced to literal-minded, empty rituals, sans thought. Judaism has laws as its substructure, but those laws have been corrupted by politics and justified defensive postures. Islam is built on rules (as distinct from laws), an uncompromising system of reward and punishment. None of these have ever stopped a war, although many wars have been started and sustained under their aegis. It is rare to find a human being that has becme good from following any religion; human beings who are of good conscience and lofty morals make religions better or at least less harmful.

Samad's **In the Beginning** explores imaginatively one of the possible beginnings of one system of belief. It leaves the consequences of those beginnings up to the readers, although it does encourage us to ponder, to self-analyze and analyze. Like any other good novel, this novel, fictional though it may be, has real-life implications. First, it keeps the moral questioning continuing, as Conrad may have suggested. This implies having the ability to discern the difference between religious devotion and moral rectitude. Discernment is a function of critical analysis and self-analysis. Furthermore, the unfortunate way things have evolved since the seventies must make us wonder about the potential danger facing the writer and those associated with the creation and publication of this book. One has to look no further than Salman Rushdie and his <u>Satanic Verses</u> which elicited such outrage from religious leaders who put a bounty on the man's head for having written a book that few, if any, of them actually bothered to read. After decades, he was stabbed multiple times while on stage by some ghoul who also hadn't read the book. The writer almost died; one supposes that being disabled by the attack could be considered good fortune. Rushdie has asked on many occasions for them to point to the offending passages in his book. They could not, of course. That would take reading and logic, and that takes some effort. The same fate was met by Vincent van Gogh's grandnephew. He was stabbed to death in the streets of Copenhagen for drawing something deemed insulting to the religion or its prophet or both.

<u>In the Beginning</u> is therefore not a book that Samad would have embarked upon whimsically. Most writers may justifiably object to such a statement. Creative writing, after all, is difficult in the first place; it is not often done whimsically. Maybe the statement ought to be adjusted: this novel, like any other serious novel, must have been difficult; but the subject matter adds on a whole new dimension to this difficulty. It adds the threat of harm to life and limb.

This novel, most members of the artistic and intellectual community world-wide would agree, should have been written irrespective of language, style, or subject matter. Creativity must have free expression, free space, if it is to be born and thrive. Tragically, we are all witnesses to the fact that a growing number of countries around the world are now banning books because school boards and politicians (they have become one and the same, really) do not "like" the subject matter or the language or a character. However, it is not just an issue of individual taste; rather, it is more a matter of racial/gender/religious bias. What seems to have arisen anew is the fear of new and not-so-new knowledge, insights, and perspectives. The wave of fear of vaccines, say,, is a symptom of this debilitating disease. Thought itself is endangered, and we react to all things logical by calling upon our vilest instincts. In many "conservative" states, the US itself have had great works stripped from libraries, museums, and classrooms. In Florida, F. Scott Fitzgerald is banned as is Mark Twain, James Baldwin, and Maya Angelou. Replications of Michelangelo's <u>David</u> have been relegated to the closet. The stunning sculpture has now become obscene in the eyes of foolish right-wing political idealogues while the profoundly ignorant herd simply follow. All of this is different only by degrees from the bounty put on Rushdie and the cold-blooded murder of Vincent van Gogh's descendant.

<u>In the Beginning</u> imagines one possible version of the creation of a belief system that a multitude of people have used over time to justify the vilest behaviors of which human beings have proven themselves capable . This novel will, sadly, offend a great many, but to resort to violence and murder because we are offended speaks volumes about the perpetrators of the violence than it ever will about this or any other book, this or any other writer or artist.

The novel captures the awful irony of how a single act of compassion at one point in history may have devastating consequences for all time. In between compassionate act and consequences, a great malevolence engulfs the world. Kay, the main female character, saves Mo from certain death. She nurses, nurtures, and educates him. She and her people pay a terrible price at the hand of the boy she saves.

Samad's characters are unevenly drawn. The solidity and carefully drawn main character, Mo, establishes the stark contrast between Mo and any other character. Except for Kay, the most significant female character, the other characters are drawn as outlines, shadows. **<u>In the Beginning</u>** is different in the manner in which the characters are drawn. So overwhelming is Mo, the main character, that the rest are merely tools used to serve his purpose. The fear he generates in them relegates them to mere faces in the crowd, mere mere background noise. They are expendable, exchangeable, valuable only as chorus to repeat Mo's words and carry out his commands.

In the culture that Mo breeds, everyone is there to serve his purpose, his ego, his ambitions. He is deliberate and masterfully measured in his calculations and manipulations. His language is as measured and as deliberate as his actions. The tone, mood, diction, modulation, and volume of his language is measured meticulously to fit his audience whomsoever they may be. He chooses his deity with equal deliberation and dismantles the others unhesitatingly. He includes or co-opts any tradition — local or foreign — to create his belief system.

The women in the novel suffer the worst fate. Mo's many wives serve his sexual and physical needs and are there for when he chooses to kick or punch. Once he has grown tired of or displeased with one wife, she is cast off as one would a ragged garment. Yet, they are still married to him and kept physically close by in case they are needed for one or another purpose. They are effectively banished, yet still tethered. Mo's devotees are limited to four women in marriage, simultaneously; no limits are placed on him. Even the casual observer can see similarities today in various parts of the world. Males dominate; women are made to be subservient. Of course, in the Western world — the more "civilized" one—the battle has been re-engaged. In America, supposedly the bastion of liberty and equality, women are now subject once again to the whims of overwhelmingly male politicians, the Supreme court itself being stocked with right wing politicians in robes. White robes in one circumstance, black robes in another. The supreme court in one circumstance, a tent in another. No matter, for the means may be different, but the end is the same. Again, a difference only of degrees.

The only time that Mo shows any kind of humanity or tenderness is with his fourth wife, Haffy. She is young, desirable, obedient, appropriately respectful of his stature, and she had became pregnant. It is the only time in the novel that he seems vulnerable. With the death of Haffy and the baby in childbirth, Mo cries. Such tenderness as he may have possessed dies with the wife and child. Then the rage is unleashed to confound all of humanity.

Mo's almost pure rage is more than the anger many of us feel at any unfortunate event: a loss of a wife or child; the loss of a parent in tragic circumstances; a crime of violence committed upon us or our loved ones; an act of despicable betrayal; an act of infidelity. We are angry and may be so for a long time. Our anger seems to demand revenge or justice. But Mo's rage springs not only from the loss of his longed-for baby and its mother, but from the misfortune of having been deformed; and, because of that deformity, having been beaten and abandoned in the desert by his parents. His rage springs at having been born, and it can seem to be satiated only by revenge against the whole world.

The woman that saves him in the novel is Kay. She nurses him back to life, nurtures his young body back to strength, provides for him in all material ways; educates him on business matters, reading and writing, and mathematics; teaches him about the histories of different peoples, different mythologies, different traditions; and protects him against the ancient habit of spurning children born with physical imperfections. Mo uses all these assets as weapons to extract vengeance upon the world.

Kay is the most well-drawn female character in the novel. She persuades her tribe that she be allowed to keep the boy and care for him as her son. Her people are not commanded but persuaded in what we may now call a democratic process. Grown to teenage maturity and now somewhat learned, Mo proposes marriage to Kay, she who was for all intents and purposes his mother. He justifies this as a practical, reasonable matter. She humors him with her habitual kindness, refusing to acknowledge the many caveats of his malevolence. Kay pays dearly for that mistake; so does her people; so does all the desert peoples; and, eventually, so does the world.

Samad's **In the Beginning** dramatizes one of the most grotesque ironies that life may play upon us: that our purest, motiveless act of kindness, compassion and love may yield the bitter fruit of death and destruction. In the end, she is made to help fulfill Mo's religious ambition, his very immortality. Then, implicitly, she is killed and covered over by the sands of the desert.

Ashwannie Harripersaud

TABLE OF CONTENTS

INTRODUCTION..iii

THE BEGINNING (PART I) 1

THE BEGINNING (PART II)...39

THE BEGINNING (PART III).......................................91

BIODATA DAIZAL R. SAMAD.................................128

THE BEGINNING
(PART I)

In a place far away and long ago, a woman we shall call Kay poured over books of hundreds of items—goods for trade. Each item is divided in four vertical columns for figures: the item to be traded, the cost of purchase, the price for retail, and the profit to be made. It was not the kind of thing she liked doing, but it was the kind of thing that had fallen on her to do since her husband had been killed by the brigands during one of his trading trips across the desert. He was, in her remembrance, a good man, careful with coinage, dedicated to trading, and loyal to her. He was careful with his camels, the primary means by which he transported his goods. He had hired forty men to guard the caravans of goods-carrying animals since renegades were many along the desert trade routes.

Kay's husband was what many may call a learned man: he could read and write, and he was good with numbers. Kay was also literate in the language and with numbers. He was 50 years old; his wife was 36. Life was comfortable but bereft of outward affection between the two. Life was business and business was life. There were no children to distract from the business at hand. Kay was his most trusted advisor, and she was quick to learn about things she did not know. Secretly though, she longed for children. But this was not a topic that was s broached or discussed between the husband and wife. Her longing was hers, unshared, unspoken. Although the culture permitted in exceptional circumstances, he never sought nor spoke of seeking other wives.

They had multiple tents, many bulging with goods to be transported and sold in faraway places. Other tents housed the men Kay's husband employed, their wives and children. All was well, people and animals were tended and well-cared for. It was not only that they were necessary to the business, but also because Kay and her husband were kind folk. With the husband's passing, the now-middle-aged widow conducted the business with the kind of efficiency that she had learned from her husband. She also had two or three wives of the men she employed waiting on her. The business grew apace and the widow grew wealthy.

Kay had a new tent built. The tent was to serve as a place where the children of the camp were to be educated. She paid the few women who could read and write to serve as teachers for the children of the camp. And she personally took care of the animals that had fallen sick or were injured.

The many tents were built around an oasis, assuring water supply. Kay and her husband's tent was a modest distance away from the others, but within ear shot of a raised-voice. Two guards were posted in front of that main tent. While not overbearing, the modest security was a necessity against raids and intruders.

The husband was killed by brigands in a raid upon his trading caravan. There was a respectful period of mourning, then Kay ensured that the business was re-activated. Save for the husband's absence, things remained the same. Not one to wear her heart upon her sleeves, Kay mourned her husband with stoic silence.

Then things changed. The change came from an act of kindness and compassion. Kay's caravan of 30 camels and 10 horses were returning from a trade trip to a nearby city, a three-day journey each way over the desert. Having sold their produce—dates, olives, camel's milk, pots, pans, earthenware, water, etc.—for a satisfactory profit, they set off on the journey back home. The trip was thankfully uneventful, until the head of the caravan spotted what appeared to be a heap of clothes some distance away. Curious that anyone would be silly enough to take off and abandon his clothes in the steaming desert, he broke off from the rest and rode his horse to the heap. Even before he reached the heap of clothes, the caravan leader noticed day-old camel tracks leading to and away from the heap.

The heap moved ever so slightly. The caravan leader was no hero, no fighter. He was an honest man, a trader, but one that was not easily cowed. His loyalty to Kay's husband and now to Kay was as steadfast as loyalty could and should be. But now the hairs on the back of his neck raised, and he felt a sense of dread descend upon him. He withdrew his sword from his waistband and raised his eyes to the sky, praying to the gods. He took the tip of the sword and carefully lifted up one, then two layers of clothes. There was a body, curled in a fetal position. The caravan leader yelled out to the others who were still some distance away. Five men on horseback rode towards him while the rest of the caravan waited.

The men removed the layers of cloth covering the bruised body of a young boy of 14 or 15. His breathing was shallow and the bruises on his body were severe. They hurriedly loaded him into the caravan and headed home with alacrity. They knew instinctively that he was close to death and had to be seen by Kay if he were to survive. Even from a distance, Kay knew that something was amiss. She steadied herself against bad news, her husband's murder still raw in her mind, a grief at loss that she refused to allow others to see. Formidably well-read, she had patterned herself on the stoics of ancient Rome.

The trusted leader of the caravan galloped in, his feet upon the desert sand even before the horse slowed. He told her of the boy they found and how close he thought the boy was to death. Kay shouted to her ladies-in-waiting to prepare her tent:

"We will need fresh water from the well. Fresh cloth for bandages. Herbs." Her voice was steady, deliberate. They obeyed, moving into action even before the instructions were done being given, accustomed as they were to the quickness with which Kay responded to emergencies. Many sick or injured men, women and beasts had been saved by this quickness to act.

Within minutes, the caravan came. The men fetched the dying boy into their mistress's tent. A cot had already been set up for the injured boy, and the men lay the boy upon it. A nod from Kay signaled that they could now withdraw. One of Kay's ladies lifted off the tattered rough fabric. Immediately a foul smell filled the tent. The ladies recoiled, covering their nostrils with their palms. The boy had soiled himself. Kay shouted for her ladies to open the front and back flaps of her tent so that the foul smell could escape. She summoned the men and instructed them to remove and dispose of the second layer of soiled ragged black cloth that covered the body. That done, the men set about cleaning the mess he had made. They took a fresh cloth and covered his privates to protect the boy's modesty as well as the ladies'. The men cleaned the boy's backside as well as his back and genitalia while the ladies averted their gaze. Thankfully, the shit was easily cleaned since it was liquid. The putrid smell hung stubbornly in the tent, nonetheless.

Still disgusted by the smell, the men took the soiled clothes, cleaning cloths, and bedding beyond the parameter, dug a hole in the desert sand, burned the foul things, and covered the hole. They then returned to their posts outside the main tent and waited in case they were needed by their mistress.

Meanwhile, Kay and her women-in-waiting had cleaned the grime off the boy's body, then she examined the extent of the wounds. It was already clear that he was dehydrated and malnourished, and that he had been beaten savagely. The welts all over his face and body, some of which were oozing blood, made that obvious. Kay set about cleaning, applying balms and bandaging those wounds that were on the face and body. The boy's face, she noticed, was strangely twisted, his jaw and lips twisted to the right side, rather like a sneer. He was without the traditional turban, necessary for protection against the burning sun. There was a fist-sized bump on his left temple, making the head strangely shaped. The unusual bump may be the result of a blow, she thought. Maybe.

Then they turned the boy upon his belly. What they saw made the three women take several steps back in horror. The boy had a hump on his back almost as big as a camel's. Where there was pity at the bruises and bleeding wounds from lashes and where there was disgust at the smell and sight of filth, now all the women felt was fear and horror. The boy, to them, was cursed. A child born with such abnormalities was unwanted because he was cursed, and they believed that the curse will affect their families and the tribe. They ran outside the tent muttering the names of the gods begging for protection from this evil.

Kay, too learned to be superstitious, felt quite different emotions. Towards the women, she felt no anger. She understood: this fear that they felt was taught to them by their parents, as they were taught by their parents, through many generations. She understood their need for the gods they worshipped, the many idols they kept in private parts of their tents. They had gods for rain, fertility gods, prosperity gods, a god for the sun, a god of fire, and other gods. Much like the Egyptians, Kay thought, much like the people of the big country of Hind, much like the people of the big continent of Africa, like the Greeks and the peoples of Europe. She understood and was tolerant because she understood. She even participated in her people's ceremonies sometimes. She danced and sang and let her hair down as the others did. Her husband had also participated joyfully in celebrations.

Kay also realized now why the boy was beaten and thrown by the wayside, and she now knew that the big bump on the side of his head was not from a beating; rather, it was a part of his malformation. And the folks who beat and abandoned him acted not out of cruelty but out of fear. She understood. And there welled up in her a deep compassion, as deep and pure as any ocean. She vowed to herself:

"I will keep this boy. I will protect him and teach him all that I know. He shall learn to read and write and do numbers. He shall know the ways of business and the ways of people. I will teach him the languages

I know. I will teach him about the various gods of peoples near and far, all their beliefs. And I will relate to him the stories of the prophets like Abraham and Moses and Noah and Yeshua whom the Romans called Jesus. I will keep him as my son. The world will gain from him, of that I will ensure. He will learn not that he was abandoned but that he was found. He shall know goodness and kindness such that he will spread such things beyond the sands of this desert. I vow this to myself and to you my new-found son."

With this new resolve, with compassion welling up in her heart, she set about cleaning the wounds, applying healing balms, and bandaging them. She turned him over upon his back and straightened his limbs. She put her ears to his sunken chest. The heartbeat was strong and regular, though his breathing remained shallow and rasping. She saw that one leg was shorter than the other, so that he will walk with a significant limp. She put her palm upon his forehead. He was slightly warm. She covered him with a thin, damp cloth that he may be cool. The boy did not stir throughout her ministrations.

Kay went outside the tent. Her ladies and the men were there in a clutch, their fear still obvious. That fear will spread throughout the tribe, she knew. She beckoned to the group and spoke with resolve:

"Set up the big tent. We will all meet, and I will update all. That will be done before the sun sets and we will all gather soon after. You ladies will join me and tend to this sick child, for that is what he is...a child. Take a small spoon and pour one spoonful of water into his mouth. Do this every fifteen minute. He will soon be well enough for a light broth. Do this now."

And so, it was done. By the time the sun nestled in the west, the big tent had been set up. Carpets were laid upon the ground, and cushions were placed in a large circle for the women to sit. The flambeaus were lit. All the adults of the tribe assembled. The women sat, the men stood or kneeled or squatted behind them. They awaited the entrance of the mistress; Kay was slightly delayed. She made sure the sick boy was comfortable and had assigned a boy—too young to be in the assembly—to watch over the sick boy as she had vowed the boy would be groomed and taught as if he were the fruit of her womb.

The women sat close together, each leaning on a cushion. They were dressed in colorful long dresses: red, yellow, green, purple, blue, cream, some white. They had perfumed their hair and made up their faces. They sat modestly, as was the custom through the centuries. Their knees close together, calves and feet crooked beneath or beside their thighs. These were a literate people, adherents to custom and ceremony.

As was the custom, the women led. They were the policy and decision makers. As with many ancient peoples around the world, this was a matriarchal culture. Women were the keepers of wisdom gathered through the ages. The men, turbans upon their heads, stood or sat or squatted, dressed in white or off-white robes, their curved ceremonial daggers in their waistbands. The men were not relegated to being passive. Their duty was to be guardians and protectors. They were the ones who executed the policies and decisions. All knew that policies if not implemented were useless.

As they sat, the women chatted with each other and with the men. Soft talk and the odd laugh, but hovering over it all was this blanket of worry, thick as smoke. They felt a sense of dread crawling into their minds like beetles or ants. .

Kay entered through the flaps of the big tent. She wore a simple white dress, hair tied to a bun at the back of her head. The chatter stopped out of respect. She smiled and wished that the gods bless this gathering. She sat as the other women sat, in the same circle that they made, on the same level as they were. She spoke:

"Only a day ago our caravan was returning from its trading. They found a boy, beaten and abandoned and practically dead. With kindness in their hearts, they brought him to us. And we accepted him with equal kindness. It is true that the boy is deformed, but I have decided that he will be part of us, one of ours."

Several gasps escaped from the mouths of the women around her. Some of the men wore their worry and surprise on their faces. One woman, about Kay's age, raised her hand, palm open facing Kay, her hand raised to the level of her shoulder.

"Speak, Sister," Kay acknowledged.

The woman spoke, her voice devoid of rancor or acrimony: "Mistress. You know that we respect you. You know that we trust your judgement as our leader. You are the most educated of all in our tribe, and we are all loyal to you. We all live in peace within our tribe and with all the other tribes. We all that are gathered here know that you and your late husband (may the gods bless him) have protected us and have been generous to us and our families."

"Thank you, Sister. All that you say is true and all of that will continue, I assure you." Kay responded, even as she knew that an objection was about to be raised.

The woman continued: "We and all the other tribes of the desert have always had our customs, beliefs and traditions. Like those before us and those before them, we have followed our customs. When children are born deformed, we have always separated them from the tribes lest they bring curses upon us all. Although you are blessed, dear Mistress, with great kindness and compassion and want to keep this deformed boy, are you not breaking our customs? I ask this on behalf of us all here, and I ask so that we may understand."

"Yes, Sister. I thank you again for your kind words. And I realize that many among us feel the worry. In order that you may understand, I will explain.

Indeed, we have many customs. They have been handed down through the generations by our forebearers. But we can be sure that with new knowledge and new revelations, some of those customs were kept and some abandoned as to adapt with time. Our Hebrew brothers and sisters got new laws from the Prophet Moses, which is why activities such as stealing, and adultery are outlawed. The recent Prophet from Nazareth also gave us great new customs, and all our peoples and tribes live by them. Or at least we try to live by them. We try to forgive those who have wronged us; we try to love our neighbors; we try to seek peace; we try to live without hatred towards others; and we try to live without a hunger for revenge. The Nazarene taught us these virtues. We learned. We changed. And life eventually became better, more meaningful.

Yet, there are old customs which we hold dear, preserve and try to live by. We respect our elders and treat them well when they are too old to care for themselves. We listen to and learn from the stories they tell, for they have seen and experienced what we have not. This was always so, and so it should remain. Each year we give alms to those who do not have. In our tribe, to one husband we have one wife; and one wife has one husband. We treat our daughters the same as we would our sons, and give equal affection, education, and things material to our girls as we would to our boys.

Once per year, if health and wealth allow, we journey to the place where the black stone hovers above the ground. Such a journey to behold the floating giant stone reminds us that there are things that cannot be explained; it reminds us of our human limitations. And this pilgrimage to the black stone also serves the purpose of meeting all the tribes of the peoples of the desert. We people of the desert invented the cipher upon which numbers are to be built. But we also learn new things, about new inventions and new habits which we then bring home to improve the lives of our tribes.

These are good customs; and, for being good, are kept.

There are other customs which must be done away with. One such custom is the custom to abandon or kill children who do not look as we look or as we want them to look. This custom can very well take us to extremes. What if children are declared by their parents to be malformed because their skin is lighter or darker than theirs? Or their eyes of a different color? Or their hair not as straight or curled, as their parents would wish?

If a child is born with an extra toe upon his foot, does that make the whole foot unworthy? Does is make that child unworthy of life? If we fear the heat of the sun, as we do, do we seek to snuff out the sun? Or do we clothe ourselves suitably against the heat that the sun gives? We are a courageous people. We should not live or deny life out of fear. We are a wise people; fear is the enemy of wisdom. We cannot fear that which is different, for there will come a time when we will encounter others who are truly different from us in many ways. Different in looks, in customs, in beliefs. Do we kill them all? Or do we subjugate them to be as we are, to believe as we do? In that case, the world shall be red with blood.

We are a learned people who seek to learn more. That is what makes us wise.

I have decided to keep this boy, deformed as he is. Different as he is. You all know that the gods have not blessed me with children of my own, but you all know that your children are as my own children. I have vowed to raise him as I would my own son. He will be learned and cared for.

You all think me wise. I ask you to heed my wisdom. I ask though I am decided." Kay fell silent, her eyes rivetted upon the carpet that covered the entire floor of the large tent. A minute or two ticked by. The gathering was hushed.

A woman coughed, signaling her desire to speak. Kay, her head still bowed, nodded. The woman spoke:

"My sister. I have harkened to your words, and your words carry much wisdom. My husband was the one who led the caravan that found the boy. It was he who brought the boy to you," she turned her head back to acknowledge her husband. He wore a slight smile. She continued:

"I cannot speak for all, but I may speak for my family. And on behalf of my family, I say that we agree with you and will join hands with you as we always have. We will heed your wisdom, for your wisdom is born of learning and mercy."

The large gathering of adults responded in unison. The affirmation came from the women: together they smacked their open palms on their thighs. The men, simultaneously, slapped their open palms upon theirs. One sound. In this way they validated a decision that their mistress had made, validation without querulousness, without rancor. The women rose as one, nodding to each other; the men smiled.

Kay moved to exit the tent, hugging those she passed by, men and women. She walked the short distance to the main tent, followed by her ladies and by the leader of the caravan. She turned to him:

"Tonight should be a night of celebration. Slaughter an animal. Our people will eat well. Let there be song and dance and merriment and joy. Gather those who are willing and make the arrangements. Our children should be there too," her instructions were given in gentle but firm tones. The man nodded and left to make the preparations.

Kay re-entered her tent, her ladies with her. They went back to the boy. Kay put a palm on his forehead, her heart welling up with pity for this boy and with gratitude towards her people. And yet, in a hidden corner of her mind, a dark doubt lurked, a thing that she was yet to recognize and acknowledge.

There was no sign of fever in the boy, but he had not yet stirred. Kay turned to her ladies:

"You should all go back, prepare yourselves and your families for our celebration tonight. I will tend to matters here, but be sure I will be there if only for a short bit. We will sing and dance." The ladies giggled and left.

As the sun declined in the sky, the fires were lit. The entire tribe gathered. It was indeed joyous: men and women danced to the music, the women twirled, their perfumed hair flying; the men, less graceful, stomped to the music. Children ran in and out from between and under the adults.

Having assigned the usual young man to stand guard over the sick boy, Kay ventured into the festivities. She had hardly reached the parameter when she was dragged by the men and women into the center to dance. She feigned unwillingness then did her belly dance at which she was quite the expert. She was indeed a picture of grace and sensuality, an unself-conscious gift possessed by all the women of the tribe. Yet, modesty was their primary quality and habit.

Over the din, Kay explained to those close-by that she needed to leave to tend to the boy. Her three ladies made to leave with her, but Kay stopped them with a shake of the head and a smile, bidding them stay.

She went back to her tent and bade the young man to go to the festivities. He needed no second bidding and trotted off. Kay knew this young man since his birth. He was somewhat slow-witted, but always eager and willing to do whatsoever task was required of him. She knew that he would run to his parents' tent, grab his squares of camel hide and a few pieces of coal. He loved to sketch, and he could produce the likeness of a person with what seemed to be little effort. His sketches adorned many tents. Having gathered up his drawing material, he would then run to the festivities and choose subjects worthy of being sketched. Kay smiled at the thought of a young person doing what he loved whilst earning from it.

Her spirits buoyant from the events of the day, she turned her attention to her sick charge. Instinctively, she knew that he will recover, but how good a recovery she could not know. The speed of the recovery would depend on the level of care he was given. She soaked a cloth in clean water and wiped his face. The jaw was still twisted. The large lump on his head had also not gotten smaller, which made her certain that it was not a blow but the way his skull was shaped. The hump on his back was the same in size, but he had ten digits on his hands and feet, although the toes of the feet were almost curved inward. The long nails made the feet seem as claws, but the nails can be pared. One leg was sill visibly shorter than the other.

Kay held his hands, her pity again welling up in her chest. Then, suddenly, the boy's grip tightened around her wrist, hard. His eyes flew open. In the dim of the tent, his eyes seemed to glow red, almost like red flames in the irises and pupils. Kay looked away then looked back. The eyes were now dark, almost black. Kay remained calm and spoke softly:

"You are safe now. Safe. We will care for you until you are well. Worry not. Just save your energy and you will get well."

The sick boy moved his head slightly, his grasp loosening around her wrist.

"How do you feel? Are you hungry? Can you talk? How do they call you?"

There was no discernible response, but his eyes fixed upon her unblinkingly. She got some broth and fed him slowly. He drank it all. Kay sapped up the drool that ran down the side of his twisted mouth. He still did not blink, seeming to follow her every move.

Even as she bustled, Kay thought of the flaming red eyes; then she quickly excused it by thinking that it had to be a trick of the light. She also thought of the harsh grip as being born of panic and trauma. She opened the flaps of the tent to allow some fresh air in, then went back to sit by the sick boy. A breeze gusted and music from the festivities wafted in. Upon hearing the music, the boy's face changed visibly, a frown of displeasure rearranging his entire visage, his eyes still upon her. She closed the flaps hurriedly, not wanting to have the boy distressed. Surely, Kay thought, he must associate music with some unpleasant happenstance earlier in his young life. And he followed her with his unblinking eyes because, to him this place and those around him must feel strange and therefore suspicious.

Each little thing was thus explained and rationalized.

From the sound of things, the festivities were winding down. Kay checked on her ward once more. He was asleep, so she retired to her sleeping area.

As was her habit, Kay was up at the first light and readied herself for the tasks of the day. Her ladies appeared and made a simple breakfast of unleavened bread and camel's milk. Kay laid aside a bread and a cup of milk for the boy, not yet awake. The women ate in silence.

As they were finishing up their morning meal, the boy stirred and groaned. Kay rose with alacrity and moved to her ward, her ladies in tow. She held his hand. He opened his eyes, sill upon her. She put her head to his sunken chest to ascertain that the heartbeat was steady. The boy turned his gaze upon the ladies who collectively took a step back almost involuntarily.

"Are you better? You need to eat and get well," she uttered. The boy groaned.

"Dampen a cloth. He needs to be wiped down," she instructed in soft tones.

They did as was asked, though hesitantly. Kay was aware that the fear of being cursed still lingered despite the unanimous agreement of the evening before. Long-held beliefs do not evaporate with a single meeting, irrespective of agreements reached. Yet she remained confident that they will become accustomed to the boy.

She took the flat bread and milk, broke the bread into small pieces so that they may be soft enough to be chewed. As one would with an infant, Kay tucked a small cloth under his chin. She scooped a portion of the soaked bread with three fingers of her right hand and with her thumb moved it into his now-opened mouth. His eyes still unblinking upon her, he chewed and swallowed. Kay was delighted that he ate it all.

Having wiped up the liquid from the twisted side of his mouth, she asked again:

"Are you better? You are safe now and in our care. What do they call you, what is your name?"

For the first time the boy tried to answer: "Mo...! Mo..."

It took Kay a while to discern that he wanted to say more, but his first utterance being "Mo", the ladies took to calling him "Mo". Kay got another bread, broke it in the same fashion and soaked it in camel's milk. He ate it all, burped loudly and fell fast asleep. The ladies set about their duties, and Kay attended to her accounts in preparation for a caravan scheduled to leave for a neighboring town to trade. For the second part of the day, she planned to check in on each family by visiting their tents, then check on the camp's children, then return to her ward. To Kay, it was all part of her daily routine, except for the new duty of attending to the boy. But it was all done with joy.

It was now full two weeks since the boy was brought to her. He had eaten well, but had not made any attempt at speech nor to arise from his bed. After his "mo" utterance and no word else, the ladies had taken to calling him Mo; and Kay had followed suit. Now, two weeks later, upon returning on her way back from her routine, there he was in front of her tent standing, uneven legs apart and hands akimbo, surveying the camp. His eyes seemed alive, seeming to assess all that he saw, all the tents, all the animals, the people. He had taken a large cloth to cover the growth on the side of his head so it was not prominent, but his twisted jaw was visible.

Kay glanced around quickly to assess the people's reaction to the boy. They were all studiously involved in their tasks. This was their way of not being intrusive or of not gawking, she supposed. He studied them with the same intensity as they ignored him.

Kay quickened her steps up to the boy and hugged him. He was wooden, seemingly unaccustomed to being embraced.

"Mo! Dear Mo! Thank the gods that you are up and about. You had us all so very worried. Come! Come back in," and she took him by the elbow and led him back into the tent.

"Talk to me, please. Are you feeling well? Do you remember what befell you? Will you not sit?" The questions came in a rush, but there was so much more to ask, so much more to say. The boy, Mo, sat. For many weeks this was the way it was. Each day, he stood before the tent, looking, watching, waiting. Each day, she asked questions. To rudimentary questions, he would shake his head or nod, but did not speak. Kay began to wonder if there was some damage done to his speech, maybe from a blow to the head or maybe a defect from birth.

Question: "Are you hungry/" Response: Nod.

Question: "Are you feeling well?" Response: Nod.

Question: "Do you want to visit the families with me?" Response: Shake of the head. No.

Even when she was there, her ladies seemed wary of Mo. When she was absent, they went about their chores with the same single-mindedness as those outside the tent while the boy stood watching. Kay put this down to their lingering superstition. His unblinking gaze she rationalized as his curiosity about his still-new surroundings.

Kay thought of ways to make the hump on his back less conspicuous, as she thought too of hiding the misshapen skull and twisted mouth. She designed a larger-than-usual turban that hid somewhat the large protrusion of his skull. The turban had flaps that fell almost to his waist on both sides. They hid his deformed head. There was an extra flap that was to be drawn across the face when people came close to him. Then she had made long robes with copious padding on the shoulders that almost hid the hump on his back, although the hump was still visible to discerning eyes.

The unequal length of the legs and the severe limp in his gait could not be hidden, although the robe was to be made long enough to almost cover his scandals. The sandals themselves were to be made of camel hide and designed to cover his feet almost fully. She had five such costumes made, three white and two black. New outfits will be made as he grew into his body. She thought that these would prevent embarrassment on his part. Importantly, they would make others less uncomfortable in his presence.

THE BEGINNING

Kay had long decided that she would dedicate herself zealously to Mo's education. And she did. She placed the greatest attention on reading and writing, numbers and accounts, and historical and fabled stories. But first and foremost, she must get him to speak. It was clear that Mo could neither read nor write, nor could he identify numbers. She set about trying to teach him the alphabet and learning the numbers from cipher to five by having him repeat after her. Many gentle insistences and pleadings yielded naught but a stare at her face. For days this went on, for many hours of each day.

Eventually, Kay had started to cut back on her visits that were done to ensure the welfare and well-being of her people. The affairs were concluded in the morning hours before the boy stirred from his sleep. Her trading also suffered from want of attention, and she began to depend more and more heavily on the leader of the caravan, that good and trustworthy man whose wife had spoken up at the gathering. She pondered: Was Mo capable of speech and hearing? Or was part of his deformity responsible for his silence? Or was it something as mundane as a lack of interest in learning. Eventually, she settled upon a different strategy. She would have the boy find an interest.

Having made up her mind, next day she awakened the boy and made him dress in his new garments. Her ladies wore puzzled expressions on their faces, visible in the nervous tugging of their hair.

Kay was in no mood to explain. Instead, she led the lad by the hand out of the tent. He hobbled along behind her as they made their way to the enclosure where they kept the horses, some twelve of them. Still clutching Mo's hand, she beckoned the group of women and men who were charged with tending to the animals. They exchanged pleasantries:

"Good morning, brothers and sisters. I trust you are all well," she said, her voice even.

"Good morning, sister," they responded almost in chorus. "We trust that you are well." She assured them that all was well.

"I want us to teach Mo to ride. Choose the gentlest horse we have."

They brought out a tame bay mare which they used regularly to teach the little boys and girls to ride. They spread a blanket over the mare's back and put a bit and reins made of rope on her. Kay tugged Mo towards the horse. The horse whinnied and shied away almost fearfully, her eyes wide. With no sign of fear whatsoever, Mo hobbled to the horse and looked her in the eye.

"Help him up and lead them to the practice area," Kay instructed.

One man helped Mo up on the back of the mare and led them to the cordoned off area which they used to break the young horses and to teach the children to ride. The man, confident of the horse but less so of the boy, led the horse in a slow walk around the roped off circle. Then, unbidden, the boy kicked the horse with his two heels and she quickened to a trot around the circle. The man let go of the reins, thinking the boy would fall off onto the sand. He did not. Kay was pleased: his posture upon the horse was sure, confident. He prodded the mare to a quicker gallop. The boy sat firmly, moving naturally with the rhythm of the animal.

Kay and the onlooking group of men and women cheered. He looked at them and went even faster, only one hand holding the reins. He was a natural horseman, seemingly much more at ease on horseback than he was on foot. After going around a few times, Mo steered the mare to the cordon and dismounted unaided.

He led the horse back outside the cordon as his audience looked on in wonder. Mo dismounted, handed the reins back to the man, and pointed to another horse, a black stallion who stood proudly apart from the other horses. He was a big fellow, almost seventeen hands, nicely muscled, built for both speed and stamina. The boy was clear in his intention: he wanted to ride that particular horse. The man spoke up to Kay:

"Sister, this one is too unmanageable for this boy. He has fire in his eyes. The boy will be thrown." She looked at the boy. His resolve was clear. She gave permission to have the horse brought. They readied the stallion and helped the boy aboard. The man was about to lead the horse to the roped-off riding enclosure when Mo tugged the horse away, kicked his heels into the sides of the animal and galloped off into the desert. They moved at lightning speed, his robes flying, the sand rising up in the air in their wake. Everyone gasped. Boy and horse disappeared behind a dune.

Kay was worried, as were the group of women and men with her. Did he fall off the horse? Did he just seek escape? From what and to what? They stood there and waited and wondered. Some fifteen minutes later, horse and rider appeared on the horizon, coming with blistering speed. As they neared, they saw the boy, robes flying like wings, hands off the reins, his arms spread wide, as if to mount the sky. Then, near the crowd they slowed to a walk, the boy's hands gripping the reins, the horse lathered in sweat. Kay saw a look of triumph, almost arrogance, on Mo's twisted face. She shoved her dark thought aside and found comfort in the idea that the boy had found himself or part of himself. She led the cheering. If he was pleased by her approval, it did not write itself upon his face.

Kay and Mo went back to the tent, leaving the horse in capable hands. This time, he hobbled only half a pace behind her. The ladies had set out their morning meal, and Mo fell to it with ravenous intensity. After seeing to freshening up, Kay went off to her rounds. She returned to find the boy outside the tent as had become his habit.

Light lunch and then set down to his learning. Kay decided to abandon conventional subjects like reading, writing and numbers. He had still not spoken, but there was the breakthrough with the horse and his remarkable display of horsemanship, a skill most cherished in the culture.

She set aside the books, then asked:

"Do you like stories, Mo? I have many stories that I could tell." The boy nodded in his way.

"Well, there is the story of Moses, a greatly revered prophet. He was instructed by his God to lead his people out of bondage. Moses suffered many great hardships in the land of Egypt where his people had been enslaved for hundreds of years. The king of Egypt banished Moses and made him cross the Egyptian desert on foot, with no food and very little water. His God commanded him to cross the desert. After he came back to Egypt and set his people free, they all went to the base of a mountain called Sinai. Moses climbed to the top of the mountain for his God to tell him what next to do. He spent forty days and forty nights atop the mountain without food or drink, and his God revealed to him the Ten Commandments…"

Mo interrupted, his eyes dark with excitement: "But why did he not use a horse or camel to cross the desert?"

Kay was stunned. The boy had spoken. After three months of utter silence, he had spoken! But she did not show her wonder nor her joy. She reacted as if his first words were the most natural thing in the world.

"Well, Mo, the slaves were not allowed to have horses or camels..."

"Why did he not steal a horse?" he asked frowningly, "Why?"

"Because, dear Mo, prophets do not steal nor lie. And Moses was a prophet."

She noted that his speech and the question it carried were about horses. That big black horse which he had ridden as if he was born to ride was the key to opening the doors of his mind. His mind had opened; the words released.

"Moses received the Ten Commandments which are laws by which his people shall live. The people of Moses were called Hebrews, desert people as we are, and they lived the way their God commanded them to. They are a people who have survived hundreds of years of hardships, and we view them as cousins.

"How long is forty days and forty nights?" he asked.

She took him outside, took a piece of stick and drew one stroke in the sand.

"This stroke represents one day and one night, okay?" He nodded. She drew one more stroke...that's two days and nights...now three days and nights..."

she made him count with her. She saw the awe in his face.

"How did Moses go so long without food or drink? How?" He asked.

"I don't really know, Mo. Many prophets have done it. Always forty days and forty nights. The Prophets Noah and Abraham and Yeshua, and so on. Yeshua was taken upon a mountain-top for forty days and forty nights where he was tempted by the devil with food and drink, riches and power, but he refused. I suppose it takes faith, in belief, in a power higher than ourselves. There are powers higher than us human beings. I will tell you stories about different beliefs of different people.

Mo was fascinated with the thought that a man would put himself through the ordeal of willingly going without food or drink for so long. He was also fascinated by the idea that one man could have power over hundreds of thousands of people. Kay was happy that she had found a way to break through to him using stories. And now she would use his interest in stories to teach him numbers along with reading and writing. He understood perfectly the meaning of each stroke she made in the sand, and he had recited back to her one to 40 without prodding of any sort.

Kay's daily routine changed dramatically. She tended to hurry through her visits to the families, paid only cursory attention to the children's education, and depended ever more heavily on the leader of the caravan to run the business. Her own household affairs were put in charge of her three ladies. The boy used up most of her day.

Mo had proven to be formidably bright. If his body was deformed, his mind was as sharp as a well-honed sword. He went for daily rides on the black horse and absorbed her stories, especially about various mythologies and belief systems. He asked endless questions about the prophets of old but especially about the most recent, who the Romans called Jesus. From his life and teachings had been formed a religion that was taking hold of the entire known world.

Knowing his attachment to the horse, Kay told him of the story of Pegasus. In the Greek story, she told him, there was this monster, a Gorgan named Medusa. Medusa had the body of a woman and her hair was of snakes. Anyone who looked upon her was instantly turned to stone. The boy cut in:

"Women should be covered from head to foot! That is the lesson of the story!"

Kay continued: "We cover ourselves from the sun, but do let me tell the story. Medusa was feared by all and she had turned many Greek warriors into stone. But then a hero named Perseus tricked her and cut off her head. He put her head in a bag, but the blood that spilled from her neck formed itself into a winged horse…"

"A horse?? A horse with wings?" he asked, incredulously.

"Yes."

"What color was the horse? Black? Like my horse?"

"No, Mo. It was white, a beautiful white horse that can fly," she responded smilingly, amused by his interest.

"I must have a white horse, Kay! I must."

"But you already have that beautiful black one that you ride each morning, dear Mo."

"Then I must have two horses, one black and one white."

"We shall see about that. For now, we go back to our lessons."

There was another incident that gave Kay great cause for worry about Mo's impetuousness and his temper. Kay had commissioned the young camp artist to draw a sketch of Mo as a reward for having written, read and learned his numbers so well in such a short while. She arranged the day and time for the drawing. It was to be after Mo had gone for his morning ride, and just after they had finished their morning meal. Mo would be relaxed, the ride ridding him of his restlessness and the meal putting him in a patient frame of mind. She made sure that Mo was dressed for the occasion, with his specially designed robe and turban, and his fitted sandals.

The young artist arrived at the appointed time with his coal and parchment. and Kay set Mo in what she thought was a flattering posture. She instructed that the drawing be done of his upper body, face forward rather than a profile in order that the large lump on Mo's head be less prominent. The hump on his back will not be visible. Satisfied with the set-up, Kay went about on her daily visit to families while the artist did his work. Her three ladies set about their own chores as they were accustomed.

She was returning to her tent when a loud scream pierced the mid-morning quiet. She saw the artist running away back to his tent, screaming as he clutched the side of his head. Mo was standing in front of her tent, his legs apart, his hands akimbo upon his waist. There was blood on his mouth.

Kay was not one given to hysteria or panic. She never raised her voice. But she was alarmed at the sight of blood on Mo's mouth and at the fleeing screaming artist. She quickened her steps towards him. He actually looked pleased with himself, at whatever he had done. Kay hugged him. He was unbudgingly wooden. She moved past him into the tent. Her ladies were there, bunched together, cowering in a corner. They were ashen, their hair matted to their heads, sweat beading on their foreheads.

Kay bent down to them and asked, her voice quiet but hard:

"What happened? Tell me what happened here." One woman pointed to the floor. Kay gasped in horror: there on the carpeted floor was an ear, beside it the drawing of Mo. She rose almost wearily and went over to that at which the woman had pointed. Kneeling down, she forced her eyes away from the severed ear and looked at the portrait. Mo's large cranial lump and the twisted jaw were unmistakable. The boy had simply drawn what he had seen. She crooked her neck back towards the women:

"Tell me what happened."

One woman spoke: "The man asked Mo to sit still, asking him to turn his head so that he can get a good likeness. Then the artist started his work. He was working fast, dragging the coal on the canvas. After a while, Mo stood up and went to see the drawing. Without warning, he grabbed the poor artist, pulled his head down, and bit his ear off. The artist screamed, and Mo spat the ear out onto the floor. The man ran out. That is what happened, Sister."

"Did the artist say anything to Mo? Did he tease him?"

"No, Sister. The man said nothing at all."

"Did Mo say anything?"

"Not a word, Sister. Not a single word."

When Kay, on her knees, turned her head to look again at the drawing, Mo was standing before her, his head lifted up, his gaze looking down upon her.

"Mo…"

"There will be no more drawings of me! Ever, ever! Never again! The whole world must know this!" He shouted. Then he picked up the canvas, took it outside and burned it in front of a crowd that had gathered in front of Kay's tent.

Kay emerged and spoke to the crowd:

"There was a disagreement between Mo and our artist. The artist was injured. Send for him so that I may tend his wounds and so that Mo can apologize. I will offer compensation. We will make right this wrong."

Two of the crowd peeled off to find the wounded artist while Kay exhorted the crowd to return to their various tasks and families. Slowly, in clutches of threes and fours, they dispersed. All this time, Mo had stood there, defiant, unrepentant, almost triumph.

Kay took him inside, dampened a cloth and wiped the artist's blood from Mo's twisted mouth. Then she saw it: a tear dropped from his eye, a single tear from a single eye. Moved beyond measure, she hugged the boy tightly. And it was as if she had squeezed and loosened something in him that let all the grief out. All the grief he had known in all his years. Mo sobbed loudly, his entire frame shuddering as he clung to her, his head upon her breast.

THE BEGINNING

Kay had not seen Mo cry ever since he was brought to her. Unbidden, tears fell from her eyes. Hers were tears of forgiveness and of joy. The single tear he shed was his form of apology for his transgression. They held on to each other for what seemed like a long time in the eyes of the three women. They had never seen Kay cry, even at the death of her husband.

"My boy. My dear, dear Mo! My darling boy," she muttered.

"No more pictures. Ever again," he muttered back.

Then came a hail from without: "Sister! Sister!" It was the two men who had gone in search of the artist.

Kay composed herself and exited her tent. With the light of the sinking sun behind her, Kay's hair, seeming darker than it actually was, glistened around the edges. She was to the men a faceless shadow.

"Did you find him? How is he? Where is he? I told you to bring him me."

"Sister, he is gone! Vanished. He must have gone into the sands of the desert. He even left behind the tools of his craft. Darkness is almost upon us, so we will ride out tomorrow to search for him upon first light." Kay nodded and retired for the night into her tent. She gave leave to her ladies and bade Mo to ready himself for bed.

At dawn she decided that Mo would forego his riding and simply relax in the tent. She in turn would take the entire day looking at her accounting which had been neglected because of her almost singular attention to Mo's education. For the same reason, she had paid much less attention to the welfare and well-being of her people. As she was working and contemplating in the mid-morning, the men returned. They had skirted beyond the parameters of the encampment, but had found no trace of the artist. They had returned and made to check back with his mother and father as to whether he had returned. Their tent was empty. They too had packed their belongings and had left. The men reported all to Kay.

Wordlessly, she returned to her practical and thoughtful assessment of her trading business and of the general welfare of the good folks in her camp. She wondered at it, that in such a short period, instead of a constant stream of folks wanting to be part of her encampment, now folks were leaving. This last concerning the young artist and his family was the most recent and the most keenly felt. She felt herself guilty, thereby exempting Mo of all responsibility. Her attention had been split in too many ways. It was not that she had become poor. Far from. But the gradual reversal of good fortune and stability had her worried for her people.

The education of her Mo, her dear boy, was still to be her priority, but that was to be balanced with attention to business and to the welfare of all in the camp. He will continue to hear of stories and histories, to read and write, and do his numbers. He was quick of mind, and that would quicken the process of his growth. Mo had started to take an interest in the business, learning the ins and outs of the trade and about schedules. It was almost a passive interest, but there was interest. One day, he will inherit the leadership of her dear people. She grew optimistic about the future.

Five years passed.

THE BEGINNING
(PART II)

And so it was that five years passed by, the business went on a gradual decline; with Kay's people inexplicably leaving in drips without customary goodbyes. Mo continued to devour each story told him, drinking in all the behaviors, habits, and movements of people and animals. He seemed most interested in the idea of a single deity with one prophet in control of the message from a singular deity. The man from Nazareth, especially, whose message seemed to be encompassing the world. He continued to be enraptured by the stories she told about peoples and their histories, by their belief systems and innovations, their times of war and peace, their rebellions and their inventiveness. By now he was reading and writing and doing complex numbers with expertise equal to Kay's.

He asked Kay if he could travel with the trade caravan. She was happy that he had finally shown an active interest in things: and so, he began traveling with the trade caravan, being sure to stay in the background or on the sidelines as the men did the bartering. He observed from the periphery the frantic bustle of bargaining, unnoticed. Once back at the encampment, he privately narrated to Kay each transaction for her examination and cast subtle suspicion on those who did the transactions and upon the reports they gave to Kay. In this way his influence grew, as her worries about her people grew. He was as attentive to her as she had been to him from the moment of his being placed in her care. He noted her rituals and rhythms, her moods. And he learned to identify the things that triggered the moods, however well she hid those emotions from those around her. She was as studiously composed as she always was, but he knew how she would respond from signs imperceptible to anyone else.

Mo took to accompanying her wheresoever she went, even on her visits to check on the well-being of the families. He remained outside the tents, her shadow separate from but attached to her. He meant to demonstrate a closeness with her, his status as being the singular advisor in all things. When they finished her visits, he asked questions about each family, always out of the earshot of Kay's three ladies.

One evening, in the quiet of the night, he broke into her reverie:

"Kay, dear Kay, you have been as kind to me as any human being could be to another, especially to such a one as me. There is not a day that goes by without me thinking about that. Not one day. You have told me of many people, and you have made me into a man who is able to read, write and do complex numbers. You have given me the ability to think. You have welcomed me into your home and into the lives of your people. You have saved my very life. You have taught me that when one saves a life, that life belongs to he that has saved it. My life is yours."

She was moved in the extreme by this unusual demonstration of gratitude and affection. She extended her hand, and he took it. She cupped his hand in both of hers. He paused for a while, his words measured, predetermined, deliberate. He continued; his voice consciously modulated:

"Our encampment is growing thinner by the day, even as you work so diligently. The business is suffering and our people are leaving. I beg of you, my dear Kay—I beg of you—to allow me to join you to bring back this camp to its famous prosperity, to help you to make our people more comfortable and cohesive. More secure. This is my only desire, my dear Kay."

"I thank you my dear Mo, my darling boy. I am touched by what you have said, and I agree with you. I am willing to have you at my side in protecting and growing this camp in order that we know togetherness and peace."

She continued: "I believe in your gifts. And yet, our people can be stubborn in their loyalty. There are still those who look upon you as someone who lives among us but is different from us. For you to play a greater part in making our people more whole, they must fully accept you as one of theirs, one of ours. I see you in ways that they cannot, for they know you not as I do. And for you to take a greater role in their lives, in the betterment of their lives, they must accept you fully. As of now, they do not yet accept you for yourself. Eventually they will, of that I am confident. We need patience. We must think of ways to have them all accept you as part of my family."

He responded quickly and earnestly:

"Yes!! And they will, but we must lead them. And that is why we should marry. Marry me and I will be accepted immediately as family. Me and you…"

"O dear Mo! You have lost your mind," she replied, almost smiling. "You are so young, so impetuous. I have always thought of you as my son, brought to me from out of the wilderness. How now are we to be wife and husband? It is almost ridiculous."

"But Kay, I have never thought of you as my mother. Can you not see that it was as if you were a wife caring for her husband, although he was younger? Could it not have been fated that this was meant to be? I know that I will take care of you and I will take care of our people as you have taken care of them! I have learned from you how to do that. I have learned to love them as you love them. Although they may never love me the way they love you. But if we marry, they will learn to accept me fully because you will show in your matrimony that you have accepted me fully. And I have loved you since the day I opened my eyes in this tent and beheld your heavenly face."

She was being persuaded and he knew it. But she persisted:

"Mo, my darling, you are but twenty years old. I am forty-two years old. I will be old soon and you will be a man looking at and wanting young women. And that will hurt me badly."

"That will never be! Never! After all, there are young women and girls among our folks, and I have never shown interest in them. My attention was always on you. And I remember our custom which you have oft cited: 'One wife to one husband; one husband to one wife.'

Also, if you were to fall ill, what would become of our dear people? We will be weakened and some band of brigands can well come and overwhelm our camp, disrupt our peace and do unspeakable damage. But if we stand together as husband and wife, our camp will grow stronger and no one will dare attack us."

"I suppose you are right, dear Mo. We will all gain if our camp grows strong!"

"Yes, dear, dear Kay! And our marriage will legitimize my place among our people. Together we will seek new ways to do well for our people. Together! And I promise you that our story shall last through the ages. The way people still speak of leaders past, they will speak of us! History!"

Kay smiled widely, and Mo knew that he had won. He grinned and kissed her cheek: "Let us do it now! Marry now! Tomorrow! Tomorrow!!" He shouted excitedly, hopping around.

Kay giggled at his excitement and antics. He pulled her up and danced. For the first time in a long time, Kay felt young and unburdened, buoyant.

And so, it was the very next day that Kay and Mo were married before the entire camp. It was, as customary, a simple and brief ceremony. The eldest woman in the camp simply asked Kay and Mo if they will forever be committed to each other and reminded them that it must be thus: To one wife, one husband; to one husband, one wife. Once they affirmed their commitment, they were pronounced married.

The celebration lasted deep into the night. There was music and dancing and jollification and laughter. For a moment, Kay was wistful. She thought how nice it would have been for the young artist to sketch pictures of the celebration. Then she became glum upon thinking of what had befallen the young man at Mo's hands. She pushed the thought aside as quickly as it came. She danced away her thoughts.

Mo did not dance. He sat cross-legged, his face in a shadow, deep in thought. Clearly, this kind of celebratory gathering was not of his taste. Unnoticed, he slipped away and hobbled back to Kay's tent which was now rightfully his by half, by marriage. By the time Kay returned, he was fast asleep.

When she awoke, Mo was gone. He went to each tent and told the men to meet him by the coral where they kept the horses. The men and women who tended the horses were already there. He shouted:

"Women! Go back to your tents!"

The women, puzzled, left. The other men gathered, and Mo addressed them:

"I want you all to prepare the caravan; the goods for trade; the animals; yourselves. Tomorrow we will make a trading trip."

The men looked at each other, as puzzled as were the women that had been dismissed. One man spoke up:

"Mo, it takes days to plan and prepare for a journey. Days! This that you ask of us cannot be done by tomorrow."

Mo's ire rose. He hobbled up to the man who had spoken, his face just one inch away from the man's.

"You will learn this: Never call me that again! Never! Since I am now the leader of this encampment, you can call me 'Brother' or 'Master.' Is that clear? There will be new rules here. I will convey to you the rules; you will obey them!"

The man spoke again: "But that is not how our Sister does it. Nor did her husband before he passed away."

"I am Kay's husband now. I am in charge now, and my new rules are to be obeyed. No arguments, no discussions! If there is disobedience, I will throw you and your family out into the sands with just the clothes on your backs!"

The men, quite unaccustomed to this rude behavior, turned away and did as they were told. They went to Kay's tent, hoping she had arisen. She had, so they called upon her and reported what had transpired. Kay listened sympathetically. She asked of Mo's whereabouts and learned that he had gone off riding, then she said by way of explanation:

"My brothers, do not be alarmed. Mo is simply anxious to prove that he can play a part in improving our business and helping with the growth of our camp. I will ask, but I am sure he has a plan. Please do as he says, and I promise to discover his thinking."

The men, reassured, began to make hurried arrangements for the trading trip the next day. Kay awaited Mo's return and questioned him. "Oh that," he responded flippantly, "was just to show the men that we will have new ideas, and that it will all be for their good and for the good of their families. I was also sure to let them know that we needed greater discipline when we go about our tasks." He failed to mention the manner in which he treated both the women and the men. To Kay's face, he was ameliorative; and he deliberately withheld the whole truth. He did not mention that he had threatened one of the men and his family with expulsion from the camp.

"That is good, Mo. But please be kind to them. They have been loyal for many years, and they have been kind to me. It is our duty to be kind in return."

Mo nodded and went about his breakfast. Kay left to make her habitual visits to the families. She kept in mind that she could now dedicate more time to this while Mo learned about the trade. More importantly, he was learning about dealing with people, so she must be vigilant while still giving him room to employ what he said were new methods.

The next day, Kay saw off the caravan. Mo was aboard his black stallion, his seat as sure as always. The rest of the caravan seemed to be in a state of half-readiness, but off they went. In her mind, she wished them good luck. They were heading for a nearby city, barely half a day's journey away.

Once the caravan arrived in the nearby city, Mo put the most ill-suited man in charge. On his previous trips before the marriage, he had always remained on the periphery of things, not wanting to call attention to himself, but always visible in the background. This time was different: he vanished completely.

Mo had ridden off to the poorer and most populous parts of the city. He knew that these many people huddled together in small places were easily lead. He also knew that the poor and poorly educated were the most susceptible to his way of thinking. He knew he needed money to buy tangible things to give to them—food, clothes, stuff—to buy their faith in him. It was an investment in his future plans. This is where his core of followers will be spawned, from this very rabble. He needed the business that Kay and her husband had built up over many years. The business must expand by any means possible, and he knew how to do it. At the marriage celebration, this is what he was thinking about; he was formulating a plan, and this marriage was the opening gambit.

Having left the trading to others, he had ridden in to this part of the city. He was a studious picture of magnificence: the high-stepping magnificent black stallion; the rich flowing robes of the sure-seated rider; the turban drawn across the lower face; the glowing red eyes of the rider. He brought the stallion to a halt, its right front hoof pawing the ground. Flocks of people gathered at the mysterious sight. He hushed the clamor simply by raising his hand, palm forward. He addressed them:

"I am here for you! I will release you from this poverty and this misery! I am the messenger of God, the one true God. You must worship him by following his messenger. Me! He speaks through me, but you must follow his rules passed onto you through me. Heed and behold or be doomed in life and in death! I shall return soon. Heed and behold the messenger!"

Then he had the horse rear on its hind legs, wheeled and galloped away. The people stood for hours gaping at the wondrous sight and wondering at the commands. Mo already had them enthralled. His myth had begun.

He slowed the horse to a walk upon approaching the market place where he had left the caravan. He stopped and looked on from a distance at the thin trickle of bartering being done. They were ill-prepared; he knew they would be. The timing was off, as he knew it would be. The goods were inadequate, as he knew they would be.

He caught the eye of the man he had put in charge and signaled that they should wrap it up. They did that in short order and set off back to the camp. Mo remained some distance behind the rest, as if to dissociate himself from the caravan. The men were clearly despondent; to them, Mo was strangely elated. After they had cleared the city, Mo re-joined the rest, but as another caravan going in the opposite direction came into sight, he galloped off in their direction.

He quickly identified the leader of the other caravan, and making himself out to be new to the business, asked many questions in deferential tones: Who was the owner of this caravan? Would the owner be willing to share his wisdom to one such as he who is trying to start his own business? How far away was their encampment? What manner of goods were most profitable and what most in demand? How many men accompanied the caravan? Did they have men hired for the security of the caravan, since he had heard that there were certain dangers that may befall caravans? How long did their journey last and which routes were the shortest and safest? Did women accompany them on their journey? Mo explained that he asked this only because he was recently married and would like if his wife came along.

The leader of the caravan was an affable and polite man, and he readily answered Mo's questions. The man was pleased that a person as young as Mo was willing to make a way in the world for himself. Both expressed a hope to meet again either on the trail or in the marketplace of one of the cities. After he had gotten all the answers he needed, he thanked the man effusively and trotted away. He caught up with his caravan as they were about to enter the encampment. He shouted vague orders to the ill-suited man he had put in charge, left his horse to be tended and hobbled off to Kay's tent.

"How did it go, dear Mo?"

"No talk of business now," he said good humoredly. "Let us rid ourselves of your women."

"But why…?"

"Just do it. Tell them to go for the day."

She hustled the women away, almost amused at his sudden manly tone: "You seem in good spirits, and I am left to wonder why."

"Because you are my wife and because your husband has spoken," he responded, a laugh in his voice. "Now come here!"

They had not been intimate since they got married, but that was about to change . He disrobed, took her to her sleeping section and lifted up her garments. Their intimacy was more of an attack, as brutal as it was brief. Then he rolled over onto his side and slept. Kay lay there, gazing at the tent top. Her mind drifted to her late husband: his tenderness, his kisses, his care. How different this is, but she put it all down to Mo's youth and inexperience. She got up and busied herself with chores.

She was updating her business numbers when she felt his eyes upon her. She turned in his direction. He beckoned with his index finger for her to come to him. She did, and he did as he had done before, save that this time he was almost violent. It was just as brief as before, but this time he turned on his back and spoke:

"We did not do well today in the city. These men in this camp are lazy, and they have no discipline. They must learn! They do as they please and when they please. You have spoiled them!"

THE BEGINNING

"Dear Mo," she objected gently, "they treat me but with respect and they do as I bid them do, willingly."

He sat up, his legs crossed: "Respect for you is not enough. For much of the day they sit around idly. They come whenever they want, and they leave at their pleasure. Our business will be no more if this continues. Our camp will fade away without a trace, and we shall be forgotten in history. Things will change from now on."

"What kinds of changes do you think we should make?"

"I will ensure that the men are more disciplined. If they do not follow the rules, they will be punished and told to leave. The women offer distractions and temptations to men. They will be told how to dress, to hide their hair and faces. They too will be given specific duties."

"But, dear Mo, these are our people. Many of them have been here since childhood, some for many years. We cannot just expel them. Thus far, they have been loyal to us." She kept quiet about his plans for the women, choosing to speak more generally about the welfare of the camp itself.

"I understand, Kay. But long service is not necessarily good service. If they are threatened with expulsion, they will work harder to stay. At any rate, should they leave, it will be easy to find new people. Our camp will grow, our business will blossom and be a beacon in the desert. The two of us will be the stuff of stories through the ages, my beloved Kay. I know this and you as my wife must believe and submit."

Although his use of the word "submit" made her uneasy, it was difficult for her to raise an argument. He was so endearing in one sentence and then hardened in the next. She decided to acquiesce, although much of what he said and the manner in which he said it, were to her objectionable.

Over the next months, Mo established a pattern. He went out with each caravan, richly garmented on his black horse. On the journey to and from the camp he broke off upon seeing any another caravan. He took note of how well appointed they were, how manned, how many animals, how rich in goods. With charm, he found out routes and times and places they travelled. The mask always hid his misshaped lower face, and he never dismounted from the stallion so his hobble was not apparent. Upon arrival at each marketplace in each city or town, he vanished, seeking out the masses, the charm replaced by commanding tones, spreading his message, his myth, his rules for a new way of life and living.

Kay had told him stories of the age-old custom of the desert peoples which had them travel from near and far to visit the enormous square black stone that mysteriously floated in the air. Mo was intrigued. He planned to make the journey under the pretext of trade. Meanwhile, since he had to speak to and ask questions of people at eye level in order to listen and preach to them, he had chosen to carry a staff much like Moses about whom Kay had spoken often and about whom he himself had later read. He thought the staff made his hobble less prominent, making it seem as if he had injured his leg. And, after all, the staff gave him the appearance of having the dignity of a shepherd. For the preaching, he assumed the language, tone and tenor of Yeshua or Jesus, although Mo gave him a different name. His sermons, though, were much more fiery than his predecessor's, with more intractable rules and more talk of dreadful punishments to come if there was disobedience or refusal to submit.

In mere months, he had established a core of believers in the smaller surrounding cities. Back at the camp, he was a constant and threatening presence. The men were worked to exhaustion, only being afforded time for prayer. He had decreed that they must pray five times per day at the very least. He showed them the manner in which to pray and what to say, how to sit, and half bow, and how to prostrate themselves. He showed them how to cup their hands in supplication, palm upward, in the fashion he had learned was the custom of the Romans. He even dictated how they must render themselves clean before they prostrate themselves before his God. It was not much different from how the desert peoples had always cleansed themselves, given the scarcity of water in the desert: Wash the hands and face, passing the wet hands over the head to the back of the neck and into and behind the ears, then the feet, between the toes and under the feet. Anywhere that the desert sand would lodge itself. The major difference was that while they were doing their ablution, they had to recite the name of God proclaiming His greatness. At the same time, they were compelled to invoke the name of Mo.

Nothing too new, except that this was decreed to be done mandatorily five times per day. The entire camp was to gather in the big tent, now permanently up, on Fridays at a prescribed time, the entire gathering made to turn in the direction of the big, black floating stone, the focal point. Attendance was mandatory for men as for women on Fridays, save that women were forbidden from entering the tent and had to prayer in the same fashion, but outside and unseen by the men. Mo ensured by pressuring the men, that women were to be fully covered in order that they offer no distractions and temptations to men. The prescribed color of garments for women was black, or dark grey. Bright colors like red, yellow, and bright green were forbidden. Medusa was on his mind; in his mind, every woman was Medusa. Mo was still formulating his rules for women; and he was formulating the forms of punishment for any infraction of those rules.

In all his years, he had been resentful of the leadership role women played in desert societies. He secretly resented Kay for seeing him at his weakest, for being the dominant force among her people, and that resentment was manifest when they were intimate. That resentment grew with each passing day.

He decreed that only men can lead prayers. He trained them himself, and they were to teach others in the identical way of worship. Each Friday, which he declared to be the Sabbath, the appointed religious leader of each community was to deliver a lecture on the virtues of this way of life and of the evils of any other, and the horrific penalties for breaking the rules, punishment on earth and in heaven. There was to be no dancing and no woman should be in the company of men, irrespective of the social event. Women who were stricken by what he called "the woman's monthly curse" were forbidden from cooking and from sleeping in the same bed as the husband. They were dirty and should isolate themselves. They were also forbidden from riding any animal.

Mo was fully aware that his rigid rules could breed rebellion. The mandatory multiple prayer times broke the day into pieces and prevented any kind of organized efforts at agitation. He had read of the Hebrew ways of fasting, of the times of Passover; and he had read of the followers of the teachings of the man from Nazareth fasting during a period they called Lent; the people of Hind also fasted, but all of these forms of fasting were not severe enough for Mo. Giving up one thing to eat or drink for a brief period would not drain much strength from those who would rebel or disobey. Fasting was decreed to be of one full month in the year;

it forbade eating or drinking of any sort from sunrise to sunset. Those too old or sick to even consider revolt were exempt from this rigid fasting. Women who had their monthly bleeding were forbidden from fasting since they were "unclean". All fermented liquors were forbidden. Drunkenness gave courage, even though temporary in nature.

The entire camp was made to witness the kind of punishment meted out to those that disobeyed. One man was caught drinking fermented spirits. Another man reported him to Mo, hoping to ingratiate himself to the new leader. The drunk man was stripped naked and tied to a stave in the ground. He was left there for a day and a night. Men, women and children were commanded to watch the man being burned by the sun through the day. Mo ordered that he be given neither food nor water. At night the people were told to go to their respective tents and return the next day at first light.

At first light, Mo surveyed the gathered crowd and spoke:

"I do not do this to please myself. I am as kind as anyone in this camp. Anyone!" he turned and gazed at Kay.

"I do this because the one true God speaks to me. He gives his rules and bids me to get people to submit to those rules. This that you see is what happens to those who disobey the words of the messenger who delivers the will of the one true God. Look! And Learn!"

He had arranged a group of men to administer the lashing that was about to begin. A smaller group had dragged the man and tethered him to the stave. Fear bred obedience, subservience.

When the first dozen lashes landed, the poor tethered man screamed. The whole desert rang from that cry. One child, a girl of six or seven, hid her head behind her mother's garment. Mo noticed, hobbled up to the child and tugged her head in the direction of the man being beaten. He shouted at the child:

"Do not look away! Look!! Or else your father and mother will be next!"

The child whimpered and looked. Fear bred obedience, submission.

The lashing continued for hours. The poor man had long lost consciousness, but Mo told the men to continue. They did, until there was hardly any skin or flesh covering his bones. He died and was left tethered for the desert birds to feed upon.

A nod of his head signaled that they had Mo's permission to disperse. The people of the camp left, the faces of men and women and children stained with tears, their heads hung in grief and eyes wide with horror. And shame.

Kay headed back to what she still thought of as her tent. She waited for Mo to appear. He appeared as darkness fell, seemingly pleased with himself. As if by accident, two things had occurred to him. First, he now realized the power of having people police each other. He will use that to maintain fear. The second was his use of the word "messenger". He had used it without giving it any thought. But he was now in love with the word, the title. He will refer to himself from now on as "The Messenger", the "Last Prophet of the one true God". He was indeed pleased with himself. She addressed him, her voice even:

"Why did you do that? That was a good man. He did not deserve it. No man, no woman deserves that. No one deserves such cruelty. It is not the way of our people. What kind of god would will such cruelty?"

He moved quickly towards her. The slap rang out like a shot in the dark. She was too shocked to scream, but reeled backward from the blow. He hit her again and she fell. Mo kicked her in the chest and stomach and head. Kay curled up and wept. He bent down to her and took her by the hair, dragging her to his bed. He lifted up her dress and ravaged her, this time with uncontrolled violence.

Satiated, he got up and said, "You will never question me again. I am the Messenger and you are just one of my servants. My God has spoken to me and He wills it that a man can have four wives and that a man can divorce his wife by saying 'I divorce you!' three times. You must submit." With that, he hobbled out of the tent.

Kay wept. She wept for her dead husband, for herself, for her people. She had brought this upon them all. She wept until the sun rose. Her ladies had not appeared at first light as they would usually. She was thankful that they would not see her in this condition of battery and humiliation. That sense of gratitude would soon evaporate. She glanced across at Mo's disheveled bedding. He was gone. It was strangely still abroad in the camp, without the tell-tale bustle of morning activity.

She quickly put on her head and face covering, this new way that Mo commanded that women dress themselves. Then her long drab dark grey robe was dragged on. Her face and shoulders and arms hurt, and her abdomen bruised and discolored. Kay pushed her head cautiously through the flaps of the tent, afraid that Mo would be lurking somewhere nearby. Clearly, he was not above humiliating her in public. He had had no hesitation about having that man beaten to death before the whole camp, and none at having beaten, kicked and violated her last night. No hesitation. No remorse. She was abandoned and terrified.

Then she noticed: the camp was almost abandoned. The people had fled in fear, the people whom she had failed to protect. Kay withdrew back into the tent, distraught. She would give anything to hear again the clamor of morning activity: the sound of animals anxious for their morning feeding; the yelps and laughter and cries of children; the sounds of domestic activity from women; and sound of camp work from men. Overnight, they had packed their belongings and disappeared into the cold desert air. Where would they go? They had fled from the random cruelty on display yesterday, from the certainty that they too would be destined to being tied to a stave and being beaten until the skin and flesh were torn from their bodies, their corpses left for buzzards.

Kay's three ladies had left too, their tents empty…like hers. Her heart longed for her kind husband. And she grew angry at what she had caused to befall them all. Yet, she had meant well. She had cared for and was kind to the malformed boy. She had nursed him back from death's certain door. She had fed and clothed him and offered him a home. And she had made him literate and good at numbers, made him knowledgeable about histories and cultures, about the ways of peoples even beyond this land, and she had married him. She had married a monster. And now he was using all of this in cruel ways. He was using all that she had taught him for the opposite purpose of why she taught him. Her people were already suffering, and she knew in her soul that there was more suffering to come, more than she can even begin to contemplate. "I have," she thought aloud, "let loose a contagion upon the world." She felt broken.

And she knew now that his rage was as deep and wide-spread as any she had known or read about: rage at his deformities; rage at being rescued and cared for; rage at those who were born whole; rage at the people of the camp, especially the women; rage at the world itself. Kay knew, yet could not understand.

Mo had seen the almost-empty camp even before day-break, its people gone as if they were ghosts. There were odd items like flotsam and jetsam from a ship smashed to wreckage in this sea of a desert. The items spoke of a hurry born of panic, strewn as they were upon the desert floor. He will re-populate this camp, but only with believers. This camp, he thought, will be the base of his new religion of which he will be the prophet. He will be wealthy, and that wealth will help to spread his influence. Influence beyond the desert and it peoples, influence that would blanket the earth forever. There was work to be done, and he resolved to do it, fueled as he was with rage, revenge, and ambition.

He got his wooden staff and his horse and rode off, his plan fully formulated. He will make of this camp a colony, a colony of believers in him and his cause, and his god. He visited all the small towns and cities where he already had followers. He ordered them to gather their families, animals and such meager belongings as they had. They were to head for their new home. This was a hardened set of men, scoundrels and vagabonds, thieves and pickpockets, but they were believers and would follow him to the ends of the world. If so ordered, they would kill for him.

They traveled in a large convoy the very next morning. Mo — now the Messenger — in the lead, proud on his high-stepping black stallion. He still caste his eyes upon other passing caravans, but did not ride off to gather information. By mid-morning his caravan landed at the camp. They stabled the animals and set themselves up quickly. Mo shouted a torrent of orders. When they seemed to be finished, he called together all whom he had appointed to be leaders — in prayers and in their society. To one, he instructed:

"Get your men and women to set up a small tent next to mine."

To five others: "You will go back out tomorrow at first light and buy arms, long swords, knives, slings, and so on. Be back by nightfall."

To the remaining: "Get every available man and boy to clean our colony. The one true God insists to me that our places be clean."

And to all: "The women and girls must remain in their tents. If they venture out of their tents, they must do so only if the husband permits. They must be covered from head to foot. Only their hands and feet may be exposed. And never forget the times our God has established for prayers five times each day. Wherever you are, whatsoever you are doing, you are commanded to stop and bow down. If water is not available for ablution, use sand to cleanse yourselves. We will all be wealthy, God willing. Now go!"

"Yes, O Messenger!" they answered in chorus, as well-trained soldiers would. As they filed out, he stopped one of the men.

"You remain." The man stood still.

"How old is your daughter?"

"Sixteen, O Messenger."

"Good. Does she dress as women are supposed to according to the command of the one God? Does she pray as she should? Five times per day? Does she cook and serve as women should? Is she ready to obey the Messenger of the one true God?"

"Yes, O Messenger, she is obedient. She will serve you and our one true God. She will bear your sons."

"Good. She is now married to your Master. She will be wife and servant to me. Tell her now that she has been honored. She has been chosen. Let her be anointed with sweet oils, and bring her to my tent tonight."

"O Messenger! You have indeed honored my house. I am grateful. She will be brought to you as your wife."

"Good. Now go to your task." The man, now joyous, bowed and left.

The Messenger sat alone for a while, thinking, charting his next move, and the next, and next five other moves. As the sun was beginning to set, he stood up, stretched and yawned. Then he limped over, staff in hand, to the tent that was Kay's, once upon a time.

It was dark in the tent; Kay could not muster the energy to light the lamps. The Messenger lit the lamps and looked down on her, his crooked jaw jutting into the air.

"Woman! Arise and spread new sheets on your sleeping place. I have a new wife coming onto me, as is my right by the words of the one true God."

Kay lay there for a while, then saw the staff come up in the air. She moved and spread new bedding, wordless. Before long, there was a muted hail from outside the tent. The Messenger recognized the voice as the man to whose daughter he had decided to wed. He opened the flap of the tent, nodded to the man and beckoned to the girl to enter. She was fully covered, as was required by the Messenger's decree. She entered, eyes downcast. He pointed to a cushion, motioning for her to sit. She was tremulous, quivering in fear. Kay looked on at it all, smelling the terror in the girl. Mo admired the awe he inspired. He sat saying nothing.

In the thickness of the silence, the Messenger snapped his finger. The girl started, almost looking up. He signaled for her to remove the mask that covered all but her eyes and to remove her head covering. He said not a word. Kay continued to sit on her bedding, quiet tears running down her cheeks. She felt no jealousy at all; she was consumed by pity for the girl. The girl, not really pretty, had a pleasant, kind face and long brown hair. Mo looked at his new wife, assessing, almost measuring, almost counting. He glanced at Kay to assess her reaction. He liked all that he was seeing, all that he would soon devour.

Still silent, he pointed for her to go to Kay's bed. Kay shifted over to make space for the still shivering girl. The Messenger came, lifted up the girl's dress and satisfied himself with the same brevity and violence as he had done with Kay; she, now relegated to the third person in the bed and promoted to being the first wife, turned her back as Mo was having his way with the girl. She was passive, the girl. She made no noise and did not move. Satisfied at his brief entry and exit, he rolled over between the two women and slept. Kay raised her head to look at the girl and their eyes met. Wordlessly, by a meeting of eyes, they commiserated with each other. In an hour, the Messenger awoke and had his way with Kay as the girl looked on with her unblinking eyes locked onto Kay's. More tears. Then the Messenger slept soundly. Neither woman slept. There was blood on the sheets.

Long before sunrise, Kay rose to prepare the morning meal. The girl rose with her and helped. Mo rose at first light, ate, dressed, collected his staff, and headed out. Then the two women ate in silence, breaking pieces of unleavened bread for each other. They were companions in misery and in shame. Their misery had different roots, but had an identical cause and bore the same bitter fruit.

As they cleaned up the tent, they could not help but hear the loud sounds of activity outside. To Kay this was new, for the loudness of speech and aggressive tones were not something done before, when things were civil. She resolved that she and the girl would go out walking when the sun cooled in the afternoon.

After a great deal of assurances from Kay, the girl agreed to walk with her. She knew that the Messenger had given strict instructions that women were to stay indoors. Word had got around the camp that the Messenger had commandeered a new wife, and her father was well known and one of the appointed leaders.

The two women, dressed as now decreed, stepped outside the tent. Immediately Kay noticed the small new tent next to what was her tent. The large communal tent that was formerly used for community meetings had been extended significantly. It was now to be used for communal prayers on the day of the week that Mo decreed to be the sabbath. She felt a stranger here in her own camp: the men, more numerous, were unknown to her. They were a rough sort, loud, aggressive. They were all armed. Absent was any sense of community, although she could sense in the people a common purpose. It was more of what she imagined an army camp or a camp of brigands would be.

The two women walked hand in hand, as the men glanced quickly at them and then turned back to their tasks. The men interpreted their open walking as a sign of their prestige, both being married to the Messenger. They also admired the way the Messenger had created peace when there should have been jealousy and acrimony. They regarded the Messenger with renewed awe.

Kay noticed that there were now many more animals in the corals, but there were now more horses than there were camels. This was now a different encampment than that which was created by her husband and herself. Maybe the whole desert—even the whole world might be twisting into a new shape.

When they arrived back at the tent, there were guards at the front and back of the tent. Kay's belongings had been put into the small tent close to Mo's. She was now abandoned, yet felt relieved at that abandonment. The relief she felt was that of a newly freed prisoner. She grasped the hand of the second wife, the new prisoner, as if she would convey hope, strength.

The Messenger was now prepared for the execution of his new plan. He had the type of men he needed in the numbers that he needed. He had acquired the weaponry he needed and the horses he needed. He also knew the routes and times and direction of dozens of trade caravans. And he knew if or how well they were guarded. He called the leaders he had appointed to lead the prayers to what had been made into the communal prayer tent. He had them remove a small section of the carpet to expose the sandy bottom, and they were told to sit around the sandy square. He remained standing as he addressed them:

"Peace and good fortune be upon you!"

They responded in an identical manner in chorus. He continued:

"The one true God has given me the mission to spread His word far and wide. You, my loyal followers, will be the instruments by which His mission will be accomplished. We all know that we need the means by which to spread the word. We know that, all of us know that. We are surrounded by disbelievers, heathens, infidels, heretics. They must pay for that crime here on earth and in the hereafter."

He paused, letting the import of his words sink in. Then continued:

"You, the believers, will be rewarded in the hereafter in any way you wish. Your every wish will be fulfilled: food, drink, virgins, everything. But you will also be rewarded here on earth! Wealth beyond your dreams! Wives!"

"We must take what the heathens have in order that we obey the commands of the one true God and His Messenger. We will raid them, conquer them, shouting that our God is the greatest!"

"We begin tomorrow at daybreak."

The men, hardened further by the exhortations and heartened by the promise of bounty here and afterwards, nodded. The Messenger then told them which caravan would be attacked the following morning, the direction it would be travelling in, and how they should position themselves. They should keep out of sight and upon a signal should attack from all directions.

"It will take twelve men. Use horses for speed and three camels to carry our prizes. Keep your faces covered. The surprise and the weak defense of this caravan ensures no resistance, but any resistance must be met with death. Everyone in the caravan must die, except for very young girls. Other than them, leave no witnesses. Once you have taken the prize, ride off in different directions and then come back to camp when the night comes. The camels will make a large circle and return here. One of you will exchange your horse and come back with the camels. On further expeditions, we will use different horses. We never attack on the same day nor at the same time of day nor on any single route. Our bounty must be brought directly to my tent and you will say nothing to anyone. On tomorrow's expedition, I will go with you. I will not take my stallion. Once you have proven yourselves worthy of this work given to you by the one true God through his messenger, I will entrust each of you to lead. Now, I will draw for you your positions."

Using his staff, he drew the positions in the sand, the prey in the center of the diagram. He allowed them to study the diagram and decide who will be in what position. He gazed at each, his eyes on fire. Satisfied that they had memorized the diagram, he instructed one to smoothen the sand. Then he drew their various escape routes. Once that was absorbed, the sand was again smoothened and the carpet replaced to its original condition.

"One reminder, my good followers! Remember that the penalty for theft from us is that your hands will be cut off. That is the law."

And so it was that raid upon raid upon raid were executed over the course of months. There was some resistance by a few caravans, and Messenger's henchmen suffered only one casualty. That man was burned and buried far away from the camp, and nothing was said of it. In all, there were about one hundred deaths, necessary killings because of resistance. Twelve little girls were collected. These were placed with the families of the Messenger's appointed lieutenants.

Even while the raids were being done and the camp grew greatly prosperous, Mo decided to keep the trade caravan active. Every few days, the caravan set off to a widening circle of nearby towns, with Mo at the helm. He was in no need of the trade; the returns were feeble compared to the raids. But he knew he had to maintain the veneer of legitimacy. He also had to keep spreading and reinforcing the message to keep and expand his following. The second was of primary importance.

Mo was most conscientious about keeping the books, and he worked deep into the nights to keep the accounts, record the profits from trade, and to keep a close account of his growing fortune from the raids. He also found time to read up on various systems of belief and how they were made to expand. He made notes as the thoughts came. Kay had taught him well before she was banished into obscurity.

Mo soon grew tired of his second wife, the girl he had married while Kay was also his wife. Although no one who knew the Messenger would dare raise a question, he resolved to obtain a third female from outside the camp, probably during one of his trade expeditions. But this wife must also be chosen from among the believers since they were more malleable, more learned in the art of abject submission and subservience. He found one, made the identical speech as he did to the father of the second wife, and did exactly as he had done on Kay's bedding, now his second wife's bedding. Another girl had been honored. Mo was consistent in most things as he was methodical and deliberate in all things. He was scrupulous in his planning and it brought him joy to see those plans coming to fruition. And yet, he was expert at exploiting any accidental finding or information found by luck. He acted quickly to maximize gains of any sort, cash or kind, using such findings or information for immediate or future use.

Thus far, his triumphs had been many. He had usurped control over the encampment that was created and built by Kay and her husband. He had succeeded in expelling the camp's population of good and kind folk, replacing them with a brigand of true believers. He had established a firm foothold in all the smaller nearby cities and towns, and had plans to widen his net to haul in new believers. He had established rules by which to worship. The encampment had steadily grown in the number of men, women, children, camels and horses. His influence had grown and was growing with each new day. He was the Messenger of the one true God, following in the path of Moses, the man from Nazarene, and the rest. And he had grown unbelievably rich. These were great triumphs for one who suffered so many disadvantages. With each triumph, his confidence grew. As his confidence grew, his arrogance grew. Until his belief — so often repeated by him and then so often repeated back to him by his followers — became hardened into deadly certainty.

He now planned to make a trade trip to the largest of cities in the desert. He led the largest caravan that the desert peoples had ever seen. He rode in front on his glistening black stallion, drawing much attention. There were more than one hundred camels laden with goods, and more than one hundred and fifty armed men on horseback. It was an ostentatious show of wealth and force, hitherto unseen. In the big city, accompanied by twenty-five of his armed henchmen, he spent many days looking at the images of the many gods and goddesses the people of that city worshipped. He counted three hundred and sixty-four, the majority being female. He questioned people about them and how they prayed to each of them: there were goddesses for fertility, goddesses of wealth, gods to raise the dead and gods to cure the sick, a god of the sun and a goddess of the moon, goddesses of the constellations, goddesses for weddings, goddesses to grant health, goddesses of wisdom, light, protection against evil, and many others. Each god had his or her own shape, colors, and his or her own rituals of worship. They all made demands of various sacrifices. Depending on the need, a god or goddess was chosen. Mo listened attentively, committing each to his memory.

He observed and listened at first. Then having listened, spoke:

"Show me the idol of your sun god."

One man in the crowd hustled back to his house and brought an idol of the sun god. The Messenger leaned his staff on his leg and reached out both his hands, as if in reverence. He made as if to examine it closely, then looked up at the smiling man. Then his voice rose in order that he be heard by the entire crowd:

"This is your sun god, yes?"

"Yes, my friend," the man responded.

"It is made of clay, mud!"

"Yes."

"And this is your god who keeps the sun shining in the sky?"

"Yes," they all responded, confidently.

"And if you offend this god, the sun will stop shining and the earth will go black?"

"We would not dare offend the sun god, sir!"

"I understand. He holds the sun in the sky. I understand. If offended in any way, poof goes the sun," Mo smiled. The crowd grew anxious and impatient. The Messenger's henchmen grew tense, more watchful.

Then, with a quick movement, Mo threw the idol to the ground and brought his foot down, smashing the sun god to pieces. Everyone in the crowd gasped and recoiled. Mo looked up at the sky:

"The sun still shines! And it will continue to shine for all eternity. Bring me any and all your idols and I will smash them all, and nothing will happen! Nothing! These are false things. These are evil things!

THE BEGINNING

The sun and the moon and your lives and your deaths are determined by the one true God! There is no other god but Him! And I am His Messenger, His Prophet. I come from the same line as Moses, the prophet before me and the prophet from Nazarene after Moses.

The one true God cannot be smashed! He cannot be killed. He holds in His hands your life and your death! He created the heavens and the earth and all living things. He put the prophet Adam in charge, but Adam was made to go astray by the Devil, Satan. He created each and every one of you, as he created me. He speaks to me and commands me to bring His message to you. You must submit to the will of the one true God and His Prophet or face damnation and eternity in the fires of hell. Your idols are a grave insult to Him, and you must repent by ridding yourselves of all idols and craven images. These are things commanded by Him through His prophet!"

The people knew collectively that they were not listening to a madman. Word of the wealthy caravan and its leader on the black stallion had arrived long before the caravan had entered the city. But they were city folk, thinking themselves wise to the ways of the world, and learnedly skeptical of all manner of tricksters. It was easy for the Messenger, now prophet, to see that cynicism.

A nod from the newly self-proclaimed prophet was the signal for the henchmen to break off their formation and scatter swiftly in all directions. A few stayed with Mo. The rest ran into nearby houses and brought back all the idols they could find and proceeded to smash them all at the feet of the Messenger.

A single man, burly and without a turban, made an aggressive move towards Mo. Hardly had he taken a step, when a henchman withdrew his sword. There was a thin whistle of metal through air and the man's head fell. His life's blood gushed from his headless body which remain standing for what seemed an eternity. Then the headless body fell forward, the blood oozing towards the sandaled feet of the prophet. The crowd, fear replacing skepticism, recoiled in terror. The Messenger removed his facial covering to reveal his twisted jaw and his sneer. His eyes were aflame.

"Keep still," he bellowed, "Now, you must bow before the one true God! Now!"

And bow they did, not willingly, but bow they did. Those in the crowd who were nearest to the Messenger fell to their knees first, then those behind them, then those behind, like a wave going backward. As they all fell to their knees, the Messenger spread his arms, his staff in his right hand, as if to take flight, as he had imagined Moses spreading his arms with his staff in hand to part the Red Sea.

"You will all be saved. You will live the righteous life as commanded by the one true God through his last prophet. I will leave behind five of my disciples who will teach you the ways of prayer and the way you will live and prosper from this day onwards. You are no longer the lost sheep. You will be guided onto green pastures, and I shall return to you before too long."

With a flourish, he mounted his steed and trotted off in the direction of the marketplace where trade was being conducted. He gave brief instructions to the man he appointed to lead the caravan and, with two henchmen, started off on their journey back to the camp. The trip back was unhurried, the Messenger stopping to talk with passing caravans, gathering ever more information.

Years passed. The raids continued at a steady pace, and the necessary killings continued as part of the raids. The conversions continued rapidly, as did the necessary killings that came with the conversions. The Messenger's wealth grew to unimaginable amounts. The camp grew populous and drew more unsavory groups, believers. The rules accumulated as did the severity of punishment for breaking those rules or for disobedience, real or suspected. The price of not submitting was steep.

One of the henchmen wanted to rid himself of the first of his four wives in order to replace her while still obeying the dictated limit of four. He complained to the prophet of the wife's infidelity and the man with whom the sin of adultery was committed. The Messenger called a prayer meeting in the large tent on the day decreed to be the sabbath. He led the prayer and gave the sermon, stressing fidelity and unquestioning obedience that women owed to men. He established a new rule: no woman will be allowed to be out in public except when accompanied by the husband or brother or close male cousin. Men nodded their approval, as did the women squatting in their partitioned section of the big tent.

He recapped the rule that a man was entitled to four wives at once, and that was the will on the one true God. He reminded that women should be dressed so that no part of her body save hands and feet are visible; women are like Medusa, the female monster who turned men into stone, and they will tempt men. It is a sin for any wife to disobey her husband. And if she refuses to obey his command to come to his bed, he may punish her with blows, but never with a closed fist. But God has spoken clearly to His last prophet that the greatest sin was for a woman to be unfaithful to her husband, and if her sin came to light, then both she and her lover will be stoned to death in public so that all may see and be warned. The wrath of God is great!

Then he called out the names of the woman and man that he had deemed guilty. In the women's section, they immediately pounced upon the woman named. The men grabbed the man whose name the prophet had uttered as having committed adultery with the woman. They were taken through separate exits and dragged to different parts of the camp, all the while tearfully and loudly protesting their innocence.

The women gathered stones and any other object that could be thrown; the men did the same. The Messenger stood apart and watched, his staff in hand.

The men formed a circle over the man found guilty, he on his knees, pleading:

"O Messenger! O our Prophet of the one true God. I am innocent! Mercy, O my great prophet! Mercy!" he pleaded. Unmoved, the prophet raised his staff and signaled for the stoning to begin. With the first stone landing with a crack upon the man's head, the Messenger shouted: "God is the greatest!" The men picked up the chant, launching stones at the cowering, screaming man. The cries from the man became muted grunts of pain, then stopped altogether,

The Messenger hobbled over to where the women had surrounded the female offender. She had been stripped naked, all dignity lost. She tried to protect her modesty as best she could, one arm crossed to hide her exposed breasts, the other hand clasped over her female parts. The Messenger again raised his staff. The woman pleaded for mercy. The staff came down with all the mercy of the stones that rained down on the woman. With each stone caste came the cry of the greatness of God. The stoned woman's cry became a thin whimper. Then silence.

The women remained at the site and looked at the dead woman, now bereft of dignity and of life. Then, almost unwillingly, they went back to their tents, their self-righteous cruelty satiated. The Messenger returned to his tent to enjoy his third wife. The second wife had been relegated to a small tent alongside Kay's. He was aroused by the scenes of stoning to death, by the screams of pain, by the futile begging for mercy. Once in the tent, he removed his clothes exposing his deformities. Using his staff, he beat the woman about the head and body until she was barely conscious, then he raised up her dress and had his way in the same brief and brutal way, punching her and pulling off clumps of hair as he climaxed. Finished, he shoved her off the bedding with his shorter leg and drew a covering over himself. Before being overcome by sleep, he thought that it was time to have a third small tent built to house this third wife. Time for another wife. Meanwhile, the girl crawled into a far corner of the tent, tucking her knees under her chin, and sobbed silently. Lulled by the sound of sobs, the Messenger slept.

He slept through the evening and night, awakening at first light the next day. He glanced at the girl curled in the corner, sleeping the sleep of the hurt and exhausted. He put on his garments, picked up his staff, and hobbled over to the tent of the second wife. On his way, he hailed a boy and instructed him to summon his most trusted disciples to the prayer tent. He went into the second wife's small tent. She was having breakfast. Upon his entry she got quickly to her feet, ramrod straight, her eyes cast to the ground. The

Messenger sat and ate at a leisurely pace, smacking his lips loudly.

Filled, he hobbled to the prayer tent. His men were already assembled, waiting. They bade the prophet peace and blessing and prosperity in the manner in which he had taught them. He mumbled the response distractedly and went into the tent. They followed him into the tent single file. He motioned for them to sit.

He pointed to two of his men: "Today, you two will construct a small tent next to mine for my third wife. It must be done by nightfall. The woman and her belongings will be moved into that tent when you are finished."

"Last night, the one true God spoke to me. He warned that people were missing prayers because they were going about their earthly business and forgetting their duty to the Most Merciful and Beneficent. That is a sin. Ten of you must fan out to the towns and cities near and far. God's new rule conveyed to His prophet is this:

Let our leaders know that there must be a loud call to prayers for each of the five prayer times per day. They must shout for all to hear: 'God is great! God is great! No one is worthy of worship but God, and Mo is His prophet!' As loud as possible at the prescribed times, five times each and every day! The call to prayer will be just before sunrise tomorrow in this camp!"

"The three of you will come with me tomorrow. We journey out at first light and return before the sun goes down. The rest will remain in the camp and make sure that the camp guards are rotated and alert at all times." Certain that his commands will be executed as he had ordered, the Messenger left.

The next day, with the Messenger in the lead, the foursome set off for a destination known only to Mo. They went to a somewhat far-off town that they had visited on several other occasions. The majority of the town already consisted of believers; it was safe. As they approached, Mo sent one of his men ahead to announce the messenger's impending arrival.

Without exception and without objection, the community of believers assembled at the large prayer building. His face wrapped, the Messenger arrived to a loud chorus of the customary greeting. Still atop the black stallion, he shouted the response, then said,

"The women must leave. Go back to your duties. Men with grown daughters must remain. Today I come to honor one family," and he dismounted, staff in hand. He went into the building and ordered the fathers to bring their daughters into the building. They obeyed. Each man was full of hope that his family would be honored by the Messenger, so they jostled and elbowed to get to the front, their daughters in tow, as sheep to the marketplace. He told them all to sit. They obeyed. The men sat cross-legged; the young girls sat modestly, their legs crooked under them, knees close together, feet behind. Their eyes were downcast in shyness or awe or terror.

"The One true God, the most Merciful, the Provider, has told His prophet that he must again be wed. We know that our women must be covered from head to ankles, except when in the presence of immediate family members. But today our God wants His prophet to behold she that shall be the chosen. Therefore, the females may take off their head coverings that I may behold.

The young girls removed their head and facial coverings.

"Put down your hair," he said, almost gently. They obeyed.

And slowly, as if inspecting a military parade, he walked amongst them. His robes and staff brushed against some, and he knew they would cherish that for generations. Stories will be told as people tell stories of Moses thousands of years after he was gone, as they told stories of the man from Nazareth for seven hundred years. He grew buoyant at the thought, and that buoyancy sharpened his focus.

He examined each girl with the eyes of a man looking for the finest camel or goat. In the midst of the sitting crowd, he saw that which he knew he will choose, but he was too clever a trader to go directly to his desired object. He stopped behind a girl with flowing raven hair and bade her stand. She was of good height, somewhat voluptuous, and somewhat pretty. She was darker than most, her downcast eyes black. He nodded and pointed for her to sit. Then, slowly, deliberately, he walked to the object of his desire. He stood behind her and her father for an agonizingly long time. He tapped her on the shoulder with the staff. She stood. Her hair was light brown, almost blond, smooth and fragrant. It fell, fissured like a waterfall. She had a small, straight nose, high cheekbones, broad forehead, and her eyes unusually green for someone of the desert. She was ample-busted, thin-waisted, her skin golden. She had her hands clasped in front of her as if attempting to cover her modesty. Beneath his masked face, he salivated, but the desire did not reach up to his eyes.

The prophet took the girl by the hand, the father trembling with excitement and anticipation. He signaled for the girl to cover herself and took the girl to the front of the sitting crown: "This is now my wife, with the will of the one true God. Your prophet has chosen this girl from amongst you."

The father stood and thanked the prophet for this honor bestowed upon him, his family, and his daughter.

"Truly, God is great. He has sent us His last prophet. May peace and blessings be upon him and upon my darling daughter," said the father. He moved to the front and knelt before the prophet. He kissed the bottom of Mo's robe. A cheer arose from the rest. The

Messenger had the father arrange for a covered and cushioned wagon and two horses to ensure the girl's every comfort as he fetched her back to her new home.

Mo also had one of his henchmen give the father a substantial amount of money and had him installed as the chief priest of the newly built house of prayer. He was now destined to be among the foremost of those who spread the word of the prophet's greatness and generosity.

The Messenger arrived at the camp in the evening and took his new bride into his well-appointed tent. Unbidden, she removed her head and facial covering and set about rearranging things to her liking. He sat and looked admiringly at the confidence and grace with which she moved. Her feet, bare now, were perfect, small and shapely, the toes perfectly aligned. She put a bowl of fruit before her sitting husband and joined him blushingly as appropriate for a virgin bride. She fed him small portions of fruit, then she ate with all the daintiness of a princess. Her fingers were slender, long, tapered.

With a gentleness that was new to him, he put his fingers into her hair. It was soft and silky. She put her head back with pleasure, exposing her long golden neck. Mo fought back the impulse to bite into her neck, to taste her blood. Instead, he pulled her head to him gently and placed it upon his lap. He was aroused. He let out a muffled groan, and she felt the wetness through his garments. Without looking up at him, the girl reached up her hand and touched his twisted face as if in comfort, as if to offer assurance. To the touch of her hand upon his bearded face, he felt calm and then still sitting, the Messenger dozed.

By the time he snapped awake, his new wife had made a small supper. They ate. He said: "Come. It is quiet outside. Except for the guards, the camp is asleep. I will show you part of your new home. He changed garments as did she, the girl sure to cover up. They went outside into the calm night and he showed her much of the camp, ignoring the small tents where his three other wives lay sleeping.

"This is all yours and mine. Remember that, my dear. You are safe here, and whatsoever you desire will be yours. I know you will miss your family, and we will visit them, but you have a new family now, your own family."

She nodded with a small smile, "Yes, I understand. Thank you."

These were the first words he had heard her utter. Simple words, but to him it was like music. The air was fresh. They lingered, walking slowly back to his tent. The moonlight bathed all and everything in the soft glow of silver. For the first time in his life, Mo was content, at peace, even happy. They went back into the tent, and it was then that Mo saw his staff leaning in its customary corner.

THE BEGINNING

He realized, with a sharp intake of breath, that he had gone for their walk without the staff. He had hobbled while she walked her graceful walk; yet, she either had not noticed or she had ignored it. Neither was probable, so it meant that his hobble was to her irrelevant. A wave of relief washed over him, and he held her close. The girl hugged him back, and he moved her arm to his upper back, to the hump. She held on as if it were the most natural thing in the world.

"I want us to do what I have never done before. I want to see all of you and show you all of me," he said, almost hesitantly.

"Yes, that would be good. We must know each other as husband and wife. We must see of each other what no one else will ever see," she responded, musically, but with more certainty that he expected from one so young. To her, his deformities were irrelevant, and so was the fact that he was the Messenger.

"Take off all of your garments, as I will take off mine," he asked

The girl proceeded to remove head and face coverings, then her robes. His eyes were wide with astonishment as he beheld the vision before him. Her breasts were firm, ample, golden, and her nipples almost bronze. Her waist was slender but hips wide, her perfect feet were supported by shapely, softly muscled legs. Then his eyes settled upon the thick, soft, curly bush twixt her legs.

Mo reached to hold her breasts; he could not remember seeing a girl's breast in this manner. She took a step back:

"No, my husband. I must see of you as you have seen of me."

"Yes," he stammered. Then he removed all coverings, exposing his deformities: the large lump on the side of his head, the jaw twisted to the right, the large growth on his back, the uneven legs, and feet that were more claws than feet. His eyes were downcast.

His new wife, his fourth, reached for him, lifted up his head so that he may look into her eyes. He did not see disgust in her eyes, because there was none. She touched the humps on his back and head. The Messenger got to his knees as if in prayer, and placed his bearded face upon the thick bush twixt her legs. He relished the sensation of the thick cushion of the hairs, soft yet prickly. This hairiness—hairs on the face, under the arms, hairs on legs and private areas—these were the signs of purity in a woman. She held his head there; he raised his head as she looked down. He had tears in his eyes. He was grateful that she accepted rather than ignored his deformities. When she looked at him, the adoration in her eyes was not for a prophet or messenger or prosperous businessman. The adoration was for him as a man.

"Thank you…thank you…thank you," he repeated over and over. They made love as man and bride, vowing fidelity, gentleness, love.

"I will have no more wives, and I wish you were my first. Then there would have been no more wives, and you would be as many wives to me. The only one."

"And to you, husband, I say this: 'You are my first and only husband. I shall be touched by no other man but thee.'"

Then, still naked, they held each other closely and drifted off to a deep slumber. They awakened to the sounds of hustle and bustle of the camp. It was almost mid-morn. He did not even hear the morning call to prayers. She rose up, dressed, and prepared their morning meal. His eyes followed each move, each graceful sway of hips, each footstep her perfect feet made, each thing her tapered fingers held. His eyes glistened with a tenderness that was alien to him, his heart seemed to swell in his chest. Love, he thought, this is love.

They sat and ate, a constant stream of conversation, even laughter. He told stories that Kay had told him, and he told of books that he had read. And she, dazzled by his knowledge, asked question after question. He admired her curiosity as he did her innocence. He drank in her beauty. He felt like he could devour her up whole.

THE BEGINNING (PART III)

An entire year passed in this manner. The peace in the Messenger's tent and in his heart steadily spread to the entire camp. He and his fourth wife visited Kay's tent and those of the other two wives. He was kinder, gentle more attentive to their material needs. The raids had almost stopped, and even for the few that were undertaken, the Messenger was not present. Women now walked around the camp and visited each other, although dressed as he had dictated. The call to prayers still sounded five times each day, and most men joined in prayer. Everyone still attended communal prayers on the Sabbath. Mo's recent wife looked forward to those. She spent hours chatting with the other women, and found pleasure in telling her husband of any trials being suffered by any family. She suggested ways to help, and troubled families found relief. The trade trips continued apace, although the henchmen handled those. The Messenger spent most of his time in his tent, talking with his fourth wife, reading, and writing his notes sporadically.

Kay, vigilant as always, noted and followed the change in Mo. Even though she disallowed herself to admit it to herself, she knew his true nature. She could not determine when she finally allowed herself to see that which was before her very eyes. Maybe it was when he had kicked her, or it could have been from the day he was rescued and brought to her. But now, in retrospect, she always knew his true nature. He was malformed of body, and that caused a self-loathing so deep that it was only to be guessed at. He was greedy and narcissistic, selfish and self-absorbed, a liar and hypocrite. His hunger for power was insatiable, and even the violence and death that he inflicted on others could not quell his cravings.

But, devastating as were these traits, these were all human traits, although they were taken to extremes in his case. But what if she was just skimming the surface? What if this malevolence she had nurtured and taught and cared for and married were something inexplicable, something other-worldly that would confound the world now and to the end of time? What if?

Then this change, this new-found gentleness. Could the love that his fourth wife bore him and that he bore her be the balm that would lay the beast to rest? Peace and love in the home may be the way in which peace and love will encompass the world, the whole world beyond the desert. Surely this was evidence that she ought not to ignore, as she had ignored evidence to the contrary from the day she laid eyes on him. Surely. Was this girl the one chosen by the gods to put out the hellish fire that burned in this man who now proclaims himself prophet and messenger? Beneath Kay's relief, uneasiness.

Kay determined to watch over this girl, this fourth wife of Mo's, who seemed with her innocence to have calmed the savage beast within him. It was Kay who first noticed the physical change in the girl. There were all the signs of pregnancy which Kay had witnessed so many times before in the women and girls of whatwas once her people. The girl was with child.

She guided the girl on diet, rest, exercise, and all things good and proper. The girl, whom they all called Haffy, soon showed the signs: her hips widened; her legs grew more muscular, her belly protruded, and she began to have this charming waddle in her gait.

Mo was delighted and attentive. He heeded Kay's advice as he had paid heed to her stories, as he had to reading and writing and numbers. Kay saw the change that Haffy had brought about in him. Now she was hopeful that the child would create a lasting reversal in his nature. She felt sure that the mother and child could bring about such a change that his greed, violence, and hunger for power would be vanquished by love and peace.

It was not to be. After a long struggle in Kay's tent at what was supposed to be a celebrated childbirth, Haffy died and the child with her. It was strange to Kay that the people of the camp went about their business, sordid and mundane, as if nothing had happened. The other two wives had tried half-heartedly to help during childbirth. Kay had used every skill in her repertoire; yet, tragedy had befallen her.

Mo was outside the tent, pacing in the manner of an expectant father. He had heard Haffy's screams of anguish. The screams suddenly stopped, and he awaited the first cry of the child. Nothing came. Kay emerged from the tent. Mo knew that a tragedy had befallen him without Kay having said a word. At the sight of the blood on the hands and arms of the woman from whom he had learned all that he knew, he went down on his haunches, buried his face in his hands, and wept loudly. The blood clotting on her hands and arms, she helped him back to his large tent, put him to bed, waited until she thought the staggered weeping had abated and sleep had come to him. Then she left to clean herself up. She felt the same pity she had felt when he was first brought to her, a victim of violence and abandonment. Her pity and care had yielded bitter fruit, and her sense of dread returned like a physical ache in her chest.

Aged now as she was, she cooked and took for him food and drink that would be left untouched when she brought the next meal. He kept to his bed, curled as if he were a fetus awaiting release from a womb. Nary a word issued from his lips, and his eyes were shut tightly, brow furrowed. Was it in grief or was some new malevolence beginning to take form? As she had so many times before, she shoved the thought aside.

She fancifully tried to feed him broth as she had done when he was first brought to her, but the man refused to respond as the boy that he was had responded. .

This went on for a full two weeks. Kay was there constantly checking in. The second and third wives were too terrified to go back into the tent where terror was visited upon them. The businesses of the camp had ground to a halt, and there was a sense of restlessness in Mo's henchmen; much of their days were spent squatting in such shade as there was, squatting and chatting, chewing on strands of grass or hay, seeming to be plotting, scheming.

Two weeks went by in this lethargic fashion. And then — just as he had done as a sick boy — his eyes flew open. Kay, again, saw it: the flames in his eyes. This time, she refused to put it down to some illusion. She knew that a malignancy had awakened.

Mo did not eat. As soon as his eyes opened, he stood, ignored Kay, grabbed his staff and hobbled out. She followed him to the outside of the tent as he went in the direction of his squatting men. They stood quickly to attention and greeted him in the manner that he had taught them. In the middle of the greeting, the Messenger raised his staff and brought it down upon the head of one of his men. In mid-greeting, the henchman fell to the ground, his head split open from the blow. The blood ran over the sand, ending at the feet of the risen prophet.

The Messenger, his bearded chin raised to the sky, put his foot upon the body of his dead henchman, and bellowed:

"Those who are lazy are wicked! They are sinners because they disobey the will of the one true God and his last prophet. To those come death and damnation!"

The other squatting men, frozen with fright at first, fell to their knees in submission. Kay witnessed the entire scene of murder play out. The dread she had felt years ago returned, took shape out of the very air. She had given him life, and he gave in return despotism and death. The death of Haffy and his child re-awakened that impulse and intensified it. Kay felt old, withered; her lips mumbled:

"Woe be onto us! This woe will last through time and will spread to lands unheard of." She withdrew into her tent.

The raids on other caravans intensified, as did the number of killings, kidnappings, and destruction that went along with the raids. The Messenger's men, increased in numbers now, went about their malevolent work with a gusto born of months of pent-up restlessness, and with the need to impress their prophet and in terror of his wrath.

The religious work in cities small and large, near and far, was also intensified with renewed energy since the re-emergence of the messenger. The rules became more draconian and covered every detail of daily life:

how to cleanse; how and what is allowed to be eaten; a new and severe fasting regimen to be done for one month in each year; the pilgrimage to the floating rock, made each year for centuries before, now took on a strict religious meaning rather than as thing of social importance; prayers became hardened into five-times-per-day rigid rituals; how and when animals were slaughtered and for what ritual observance — each was made clear and mandatory; and women were placed at the lowest rung of the ladder and open to decreed abuse from the one true God through his chosen prophet, His last to be granted to the desert peoples, the peoples of the world.

Mo, the Messenger and Last prophet, had calculated each move. To him, it was simple. The frequency of prayer broke the days into pieces, so there would be no time to scheme and plot and rebel. The spying and reporting on neighbors for perceived infractions helped to keep everyone in line. The severe one-month-long fasting from pre-day-break to post-sunset without liquids of any sort left whole communities weakened and in a perpetual half-daze. Between work and prayers and fasting, the people became more submissive, the word SUBMIT becoming the central tenant of the new religion. Submit. Gatherings were strictly segregated by gender, as were the communal prayers on the sabbath. These communal prayers were invariably used to further indoctrinate and reinforce the rules laid down by the messenger and passed down to his followers whom he appointed to be religious leaders. They too were made to report to the messenger, lest they assumed for themselves too much power. Above all, the virtues and singularity of the prophet were to be sung. Each call to prayer screamed his name; each greeting, however casual, contained his name.

The worth of girls and women was made to be one-tenth the worth of boys and men. This was calculated in terms of gold and other material wealth. Inheritances were so calculated and decreed. Females, once married, became the property of the men they married, and with that ownership came the ownership of all she possessed. Violence against women was validated, but the sermons insisted on the great equality of the new faith.

In a year, Mo had taken onto himself three wives and inflicted on them the treatment he had meted to Kay and the other wives, save his dear Haffy. Once used and abused, they were condemned to little tents in the order of abandonment. None of the women gave him the son he so wanted. No daughter either, but that did not matter much to the Messenger. He needed a son to keep his name ringing through the ages. The messenger was never heard of having parents.

The previous prophets—especially the Nazarene, Moses and Abraham—were to him an obsession. The Nazarene was of virgin birth, it was claimed. Mo was more special since he had simply appeared. To Mo, truly he as the last prophet was the chosen. The date that he claimed to have appeared was declared a holiday. Songs of praise and many prayers that assuredly brought copious blessings to the believers echoed through the desert. In all songs and praises, the Messenger's name took resounding centrality. But Mo also remembered the tales of the Greeks and Romans, the idol-worshipping peoples of Hind, and the Danes, as Kay had related and as he had absorbed.

All of these prophets, to the Messenger's way of thinking, had three shortcomings in common. First, their stories had come down through the ages by word of mouth, through mere disciples. This was not efficient for keeping the records, not efficient for historical permanence. Many deeds could have been missed or forgotten. The rules may have got lost or perverted. The reputation of prophets could have been greater and more lasting. Apart from Moses, they left no written records of their deeds and teachings. He, the last prophet, will leave written records to ensure sameness and continuity. The past prophets had all suffered in horrible ways. The Messenger determined that his end will be different. As the last prophet it would not be appropriate for him to suffer in any way. No one was going to make him cross the desert on foot and with no water, and no one will hang and nail him to a cross.

These prophets of old did not make firm plans for their work and themselves to be remembered. They did not see that sameness and rigid routine were vital. They did not insist on sameness and on punishment for breaking the rules. They did not insist on established times and manner of prayers, and their followers were allowed to pray when they wanted, if they wanted. Fasting was done or not done, according to each individual prophet and each individual follower, according to their own discretion. He would not have that ill-discipline that was tolerated by those who came before him, women did not know their place because there were no rules. With his way and the way of his God, women will have to obey the rules he set out, or pay the price.

And all of this, thought the messenger, was because none of them saw the connection between wealth, power and the efficient spread of their way of life. The man from Nazarene preached love, but had no firm rules to ensure obedience. He had but twelve disciples, but this Messenger had two hundred and forty. The man from Nazareth did not use his disciples to spread the message with any kind of efficiency. Neither did he realize that the expansion of religion depended on the accumulation of wealth. None of them left written records; instead, their works and teachings were left to others to record as they remembered which was highly unreliable. He would have none of that. There will be no room for ambiguity, no room for interpretation.

Worst of all, these prophets allowed others to invade and defeat them by force. Not this messenger! This messenger will invade rather than be invaded. He will conquer rather than be conquered. This prophet, this last messenger, will lay down the rules and spread the message with the sword. He will not suffer. He had begun by being an object of scorn; he will end by being a figure of glory unparallelled.

Mo prepared to write his holy book and a companion to that holy book. The second book was to be entirely about him, the greatest of prophets. But he needed there to be mystery around the books. Kay, long beyond physical or social or economic use to him now, can be put to use for this task. He ruminated on strategy for days, remembering forty days and forty nights and Moses and Noah and Joshua and Elijah, and the man from Nazarene, and one of the gods of the peoples of Hind. Always forty days and forty nights without food and water Always alone. This he too will do or will appear to do. But first, he must arrive at a plan to magically disappear, taken by the one true God like so many other prophets were taken to an isolated place where the great message was to be revealed from God to the holy prophet.

He sent word to all of his chieftains having them gather at the prayer tent on a specific day and time. They came, each bowing low before the Messenger. He counted to make sure that they were all there. Two hundred and forty. He bade them sit. They sat almost shoulder to shoulder, cross-legged, quiet. Large as was the tent, they were crowded. The last prophet as he had proclaimed himself to be kept standing, staff in hand. He looked down upon them, his eyes on fire, his brow furrowed, his bearded chin up. He kept silent and the silence seemed to clang in the air. Minutes. His chieftains tensed with expectation or fear. More minutes. Beads of sweat formed on their foreheads. Finally, he spoke:

"I welcome you in the name of the one true God, may His peace and blessings be upon you."

They responded in kind.

"You all know that He is the most merciful, the most beneficent.

They nodded.

"You know that it is He who has given you life, and it is he who takes life."

They nodded.

"He gives you peace and prosperity through His last prophet who stands before you."

"Yes, we know. All praise and thanks must go to the one true God and his Holy Messenger! God is great!!"

"God is great! He must be obeyed. You are all His servants and His children. You owe each thing you eat to Him. You owe the life of your sons and daughters and wives to him. If you — each and every one of you — fail to submit to His will and to the will of His last Prophet, woe be upon you! Death and destruction will come to you and your families,"

They answered yes, fear now replacing anxiety and anticipation.

The one true God appeared to me a few nights ago. He was in the form of a cloud and spoke to me from within the clouds. With the voice of the thunder he spoke to me, His last Prophet, and bade me hand great news down to you, you who are my disciples."

"What are His Messages, O Prophet?" one man asked.

He turned his back to them, seeming overcome with emotion. Minutes went by, then he turned to face them, his face awash with tears.

"The one true God told me from within the clouds this: 'You are my Chosen prophet and your people are my chosen people. You have pleased me greatly with your works and your prayers and your teachings, and I have tested you by making you different from ordinary people. That was your trial.'

'You must now spread the Word to all corners of the earth that I made. You, who cannot read nor write, will be commanded to read and write, and thus shall My will be known through all time and to all people in all the lands.'"

"I spoke with trembling voice asking how can it be that I who can neither read nor write, can now do so. The thunderous voice of the one true God rose loud and he said: 'I am your God, your Lord! With me, all things are possible! Question no more! I will take you to a place where no one has been and reveal onto you a Holy Book which all generations hereafter shall read and follow. Those who do not obey shall know hell-fire for eternity. They will be the non-believers, the infidels, and woe be onto them. The wrath of the one true God shall descend upon them in life and after death. Now go, call your disciples and announce to them that which I have passed on to you.'"

"This is why I have summoned you, upon the command of the one true God. I say onto you now: Be obedient! Submit to the will of the Almighty for he knows all that you have done, all that you have thought and are thinking, and all thoughts you will have. He sees all, and he speaks to his prophet."

"I shall disappear from sight for forty days and forty nights so that our one true God can reveal to me what was, what must be, and what will be…"

Another man spoke up, voicing the concern felt by all:

"O prophet! What are we to do when you are gone? Who will lead us? Where will you go and how will you get there unharmed? Tell us, O prophet of the one true God."

"You have asked, and I will answer. You will pray and do as I have taught you. I will remain with you, watching with the eyes of the one true God. If you are treacherous or disobedient to my commands, I will know. And your punishment will be assured. You will lead the people in the places where you live. Pray. Fast. Wait. Do no business until you are commanded. I will go to where our God takes me, for no harm will come to the last prophet of God."

"Now, go! And do not seek me out." They rose to their feet slowly, each reaching to touch his robe before departing. He basked in the adoration. Then he was alone. The messenger finally sat, he sat there until darkness had fallen upon the desert, his mind saturated with that which must be done to assure his immortality.

He went to Kay's tent and entered through the flaps:

She looked up from her reading:

"Peace and blessings of the one true God be upon you," he greeted, almost pleasantly.

Not returning the greeting, she asked: "What can I do for you that I have not already done?"

His demeanor changed: "Ready a few things. Very few. But bring your writing materials and implements. We will leave soon."

She made to ask why, and where to, but he raised an imperial hand to cut the questions off even before they were uttered.

"Make haste!" With that command, he left.

He returned to his tent, ate the food that his most recent wife had prepared, and then instructed her to go to the tent of one of the other wives.

'Do not return for two days," he barked. Learned in the ways of submission, she obeyed.

Now the messenger too must ready himself. He packed clothes and writing material into a sack, making sure he had the notes he had been making for years now. He packed supplies of food and water. It would not have done to allow Kay to do that; there would be too many questions.

He took her to the corral, and blanketed two nondescript horses, leaving his now-aged stallion behind. That would add to the mystery of his disappearance. The bags were slung across the sides of a third animal, and they rode off into the night. They rode without hurry, for haste draws attention. Mo avoided travelling during the day, choosing to put up an inconspicuous tent to protect them from the desert sun's harsh rays. They ate and slept during the day; at night, they set off again.

They slept for five days and traveled for five nights before they came upon the destination, known only to the messenger. He had chosen well. The place was enclosed by ragged mountains with a narrow passage into the haven. It was quiet, isolated, and shielded from prying eyes.

They labored to erect a tent, big enough for both. The work began. Kay was charged with writing a book about the "life and teachings of the prophet" which laid down the rules of living and worshipping. The book was to provide anecdotes of the prophet's generosity, the kindness and love he showed to the chosen, all extolling the virtues of the messenger, the last prophet. Mo provided her with some neatly written notes that he had taken over the years. She was to be guided by them. As she finished a chapter, he took time off from his own writing and checked hers. Making corrections, adding stories, striking off bits that could be interpreted as critical of his virtue and divinity.

He himself concentrated on the holy book in which the one true God had revealed to him all the rules that were to be obeyed henceforth. The book was to be a revelation in its entirety about a man who had the word spread that he could neither read nor write. It was meet, therefore, that the one true God would command that his last prophet read and write. It was to be part of the story, the mystery, the revelation.

The rules were firm and the punishments for disobedience or failing to submit severe and precise indeed. It contained what he called the five pillars upon which the religion is built: the profession of fidelity and unquestioning submission to the faith, its God and its prophet; prayer five times per day facing the floating black box in the big city; month-long fasting annually and the rules for that; annual journeys to the black box; the giving of charity, with exact figures of profit margins and what percentages were to be given. Call to prayers five times daily with the prophet's name featured prominently.

As always, he remembered the winged horse, Pegasus. He was brought, like the man from Nazareth, to a mountain-top, but he was to be brought by a white horse who had a name. The horse had instructions from the one true God to take the last prophet upon its back to a mountain-top far, far away. The one true God was the God of all the prophets through time, but Moses' God had no name. Mo gave the one true God ninety-nine names. The book held that the man from Nazareth was to return to signal the end of the world and exact grave punishment upon idol worshippers and other non-believers.

The worth of girls was measured in ounces of gold; the worth of boys in more gold. The distribution of property was dictated, unequally, boys getting the lion's share. Men could marry up to four wives at the same time, each to be taken in agreement with the first. The way a woman must dress was stipulated, and the reasons given: women were tempters and must be covered. All women in the world must dress in the desert fashion. They were to avoid reading and writing. Men were allowed to strike women, but only with open fists, beaten especially if she did not grant sex when commanded by the husband. Each act of disobedience was accompanied by punishment for infractions. Punishment here and in the hereafter were stipulated for every possible infraction. The one true God also instructed mankind to think critically, but never to question His will nor the will of his last prophet. That would constitute blasphemy.

The manner of prayer was clearly stipulated, including the separation of men from women, the call to prayer, the rituals before, during and after, the position demonstrating total submission to the will of the one true God. There were rules about conversion and dire consequences for those who refused. If a man of faith chose to marry an infidel, she must convert; if a woman of faith chooses to marry a male who was heathen, he must convert. Yet, no one can be coerced into converting. If idol-worshippers refused to convert, they were either to be put to death and their women taken or they had to be taxed into submission.

There were thousands of references to the omniscience, all-knowing, all-seeing, generous, vengeful nature of the one true God, and He was given precisely ninety-nine names. Hell awaited heathens and non-believers, and blessings in Heaven awaited the true believers: milk and honey and virginal women. Those who killed or were killed fighting for the one true God were singled out as martyrs who will have special privileges in Heaven, more women, more milk, more honey.

The book was divided into sections, and each section had verses establishing the rules and extolling the virtues of the one true God and his last prophet, Mo. It began with vaunting praise about the generous nature of the one true God, how He may wrench away all bounty and why, and many warnings about punishments that would fall upon non-believers, sinners, heathens, and those who do not submit to nor praise the one true God and His last prophet. Certain verses were to be uttered upon a variety of activities: eating, bathing and other activities, sacrificing animals, even the manner in which to put on sandals. The book was extraordinarily thorough in its details regarding rules of living and burying the dead, and everything in between birth and death. The holy book was about credits and debits in the manner of a business ledger.

Mo wrote this book, and he gave Kay each section to read and correct as he finished it; in turn, he read her book on the life and teachings of the last prophet. It was all done relatively quickly, helped along by Mo's notes and by Kay's formidable education. He objected to and removed the stories that placed the messenger in a less-than-glowing light. The story with the artist was scratched off as were the caravan raids and the killings. But the instruction was stark that there be no visual representation of the holy prophet's image.

He insisted that stories be told of his love for animals, and his favorite one was this: One day, the prophet of the one true God sat in the home of one of the men he had made prosperous. The man and his family fussed and doted on the prophet. His long robes flowed to the floors. The man's family had dozens of cats, and one black cat of the number crawled, curled and slept upon the hems of his robes. It came time for the prophet to leave, and the man made to lift the sleeping cat from off the seams of the prophet's robe. The prophet would have none of it; he insisted that the cat not be awakened. He continued to sit for an hour or so as the cat awakened, stretched, meowed, and went back to sleep. The man of the house called out to his household, including his servants and slaves to witness the compassion of this holy prophet who disdained to awaken a sleeping cat, so deep was his compassion. The man cried at the sight, as did his sons and daughters and wives. The faces of the servants and slaves were awash with tears, so moved were they by this sight of divine compassion. Eventually, the cat awoke, stretched and pawed away, quite unaware that it would go into the annals of history as being the recipient of holy compassion and mercy.

The revealed book and the book about his life and teachings were completed slightly behind the established schedule which was based on various stories about several holy men or prophets that came and went. In spite of Mo's notes having quickened the process, the work was simply too laborious for a single man and a single woman to complete in forty days and forty nights.

They broke camp as soon as the revealed book was done and the second book almost done, Mo being careful to erase any trace of their presence at the site. Six days later, the last messenger appeared on the horizon of his camp, now seemingly grown larger and richer. He was on foot. There were no horses, no folded tent, no equipment, no food or water, all so necessary for survival in the desert. And there was no Kay, she whose kindness, compassion and care had saved his life.

The last messenger appeared on the horizon on foot, with the sun behind him. By his gait and his silhouette, the lookouts recognized him. They raised a joyous alarm, and all the men in the camp ran towards him.

"Praise be to the one true God. The prophet has returned! God is great! He has returned our prophet, our leader, our savior!"

They screamed and shouted. They laughed and slapped each other's shoulders with glee and relief. The men reached out to touch his garments to be sure it was no mirage, no trick of light. The sun behind him, the prophet looked upon them, his eyes glowing red in the shadow that was his face.

Standing statue-like while his devotees swarmed around him, he took time to bask in the rejoicing of his followers. All this while, he held the holy book in the crook of his right elbow, as he had imagined Moses held the sacred tablets etched with the Ten Commandments of God. He had considered holding in the crook of his left elbow the second book of his teachings and examples. Like Moses. But then he thought better of it since he will surely write in more of his teachings. He had years to live. Instead, he stuck the second book within the folds of his ample robes.

The last prophet stood still for what seemed like a long while . As the din rose to a crescendo, the messenger held the holy book above his head with both hands and shouted:

"Behold! Behold the word of God! The direct words of God revealed to His prophet upon a mountain-top. Behold!"

The noise stopped at once, replaced by a pious silence. The last prophet, his voice raising like a desert storm, said:

"We will submit and give thanks that the one true God, God of Abraham, and Isaac, and Moses, and Yeshua, The most merciful, the beneficent, the all-seeing and all-knowing. Let us submit to His will and the will of his prophet who stands before you! Those of you who are not cleansed by water will use the desert sand to render yourselves clean, as I have taught you!"

And he turned to face the direction of the mysterious floating black stone, knelt in the fashion he himself had prescribed, and prayed. His excited followers, putting aside their many questions, kneeled and bowed and muttered prayers after him.

The last messenger made to move towards the encampment, more like a settlement now. The followers made a path, falling flat on their bellies as he passed them. For his part, he kept his eyes ahead, not nodding, his long beard and chin lifted up to the heavens.

The path the followers made led to the wings of the messenger's tent. The women had had time to dress themselves appropriately and stood behind the line of men. They knew their station well, having been taught well. Before he entered his large tent, the last prophet turned to the many gathered, the holy book clutched to his bosom. He nodded and entered.

His most recent wife, the one least excited to see him, dutifully placed his meal before him. The last prophet ate sparingly, silently. Finished, he pointed her to his sleeping area and did what for him was now habit: quick sexual self-gratification. Then he fell asleep, his book always by his side. He awakened only to eat, then went back to bed, eyes wide open, gazing, thinking.

The messenger planned his next move. To maximize the impact and import of the Holy Book, he needed to spread the word of its revelation quickly and to all. It was essential to spread this new religion that he had spent his life spawning. Money must continue to be generated to spread the word. The story must be formulated in his mind and the narration clear. He needed a better equipped workforce: soldiers, uniformed, dressed in armor as were the Romans, and just as disciplined. The Romans moved in columns; his forces must be more versatile, more adaptable. There must be conquest beyond the desert. Conquest meant profit, more resources; it also meant more women. And the conquered will themselves spread the word. He will be immortal. His holy name shall be on the lips of believers everywhere and for all time, although they will never know what he looked like. The timing of the announcement of the companion book must be perfect, and no writer will be acknowledged.

His reverie was disturbed by the noises his current wife made. He had long grown impatient with her rough and noisy way of doing ordinary chores. Her every movement raised his ire. Having been interrupted in mid-thought on matters of import triggered him to make an immediate domestic decision. She would today be banished to one of the small outer tents that surrounded his. Like the rest, she will be made to wait there until he found use for her. A next wife can be found easily.

On the third day, he rose, as if from resurrection. He summoned his trusty captains to assemble in the prayer tent and await his arrival. His jaw contorted into what may have been a smile or a sneer at the story he will relate, and that they will relate to all they know, forever and ever, wider and wider. The story he will tell them will encircle the world.

He entered the large prayer tent after they were assembled. They rose at his entrance and lined up to kiss the folds of his garment. He clutched his holy book to his chest, hobbling slowly that his disciples may kiss or touch his folds. He had practiced the demeanor of a man who had had contact with divinity, and he tried to wear that demeanor today: the set face, the furrowed brow; the seriousness that came with the burden of prophecy; and above all the humility. The Hebrew Moses must have looked like this, he thought.

He stood before his disciples. They remained stock still before their chief, the trader, the messenger, the last prophet before the day of judgement. He made eye-contact with no one, keeping his eyes focused on the top of the backside of the large tent. He had seen God and could gaze no more upon mere mortal men.

Clutching the leather-bound book in one hand, he weakly waved the other hand signaling them to sit. They sat, all at once, still good soldiers. He waited and waited until he saw them almost explode with curiosity. Finally, he spoke. He spoke slowly so that each word may seem to carry weight, importance, gravitas:

"In the name of the one true God, the most merciful, the most beneficent, I come to you as His last prophet to whom He spoke. A miracle befell me, the last prophet of the living God, creator of all things, the author of the beginning and the end. Listen well and submit to His will or face hell-fire for all eternity!"

Pause. Absorption. Weight.

"More than one moon ago, I heard a noise outside my tent. I went out. And there was this pure white horse standing there as if it were carved of marble. We looked upon each other, he with admiring eyes, me with eyes wide with wonder. Then the horse told me his name and said:

"O Prophet of the one true God, I was sent by your Lord to take you to a secret place where He will reveal to you the rules of life, of ways to live, rules that will govern humanity for all times to come."

Pause. Wait. Absorption. Suspense.

"I was surprised, but listened. I made to go back into the tent to pack for the journey, but the horse said to me: 'Stop! You will need nothing. The one true God that rules the heavens and the earth has all things prepared for his last prophet. Come aboard my back.'"

"I obeyed. The horse flew like the wind, flying high above the earth, although he had no wings. We flew a long, long way, but the journey did not seem long at all. The horse prayed loudly and told me to pray loudly with him. We sang the praises of the one true God as we flew high above the earth.

We landed, I had never seen such a place before . There was water and food, flowers and palm trees, lots of green grass, and snow on distant mountaintops. Never have I seen such a beautiful place. I ate and fell asleep.

I was awakened by a voice that was at the same time inside and outside my head: 'In the name of the one true God, you, my last Prophet are hereby commanded to write!'

I was much puzzled, for, as we all know, I cannot read nor write. On a carpeted floor, I saw many quills and parchment before me. I suddenly picked up a quill and followed the voice. I wrote as was revealed onto me.

This Holy Book –the holiest of all books now and forever more – is the last revealed Word of the one true God, and it must be obeyed by all of humanity until the end of the world, called Judgement Day. Those who follow me, the last prophet, and the rules set forth in this book shall be saved. Those who do not will be condemned to hell-fire for all eternity. All people must submit. All.

The Book is written in our holy language and is never to be translated. Neither can these holy words be uttered from the vile mouths of heathens or they must be severely punished. Through this Holy Book, and through this Holy Book alone, shall the will of the one true God be conveyed to all of humanity. You shall all preach from this and from this alone."

The Last Prophet paused to catch his breath, and then sighed as if the weight of the whole world was upon him. He continued, but quicker now. Urgent.

"It is upon the command of the Most High that we must spread our faith to all corners of the world. Already, we have ordained almost all the peoples of the desert, but the world is large and we must have an army, for there are those in the world who will hold stubbornly to their heathen beliefs, to their idol-worshipping ways. We must save them from the terrible wrath of the one true God. It is through us that they will be saved, or else woe be onto them. If they do not change their evil ways by our words, they must be made to change their ways by our swords. So sayeth the one true God, the Most Mighty, the All-High, the All-knowing and All-seeing. We have been given a command, and we will obey.

Every able-bodied man and boy is commanded by the One True God to join our army to be trained. We shall be as fierce as the Greeks and as equipped as the Romans. Our God has assured us victory over lands rich beyond our dreams. Rich with treasure and women and slaves that we may keep, sayeth our One True God. It will take leadership and discipline and faith without question, but victory is indeed assured if we obey! We will invade east and west, and become as kings. Are you willing to submit to the will of our God, the True God? Are you willing to kill all infidels in the name of our one true God and his last prophet who speaks to you here?"

A roar went up from the crowd: "We will do as we are Commanded, O Prophet! And a chant arose in wave upon wave: "Praise be our Prophet! God is the greatest!"

"Now go! Make preparations! Gather up our faithful! Bring them here to our camp! We begin training our army when you return. Each of you shall command a Company and train them."

And so, they all went forth to the near and far corners of the desert, their minds on fire at the prospects of conquest, new treasure and women and slaves and power. They were diligent in their reaping of new bodies for the prophet's army.

As instructed, they each returned to the encampment—now grown to a military complex—with hundreds and thousands of recruits. New battle-dress, and weapons, and camels and horses were seized and brought forth. The training began.

The encampment that was Kay's was once busy with the noises of everyday work, with chatter and laughter, with talk of trade. That camp was now a military base which resounded with the clash of metal on metal, the grunts of hand-to-hand combat, with barked commands and barked sounds of military obedience.

Meanwhile, the Messenger remained out of sight within his tent, newly-wived again, busy adding to and subtracting from Kay's book about his life and teachings. He also prepared plans for conquest towards the East and the lands of Hind, rich with women, wealth, and slaves. Simultaneously, he prepared plans to attack West towards Europe about which Kay had spoken.

From time to time, carefully measured, he would appear on a high platform to gaze upon his gathered forces and for them to gaze upon him and bow to The Presence. There was always a distance, such that his deformities could not be noticed and that there could be no details of his features. His henchmen, now his generals, ensured this. He never spoke, knowing his silent gaze would add to his mystique, his enigma, his superiority. All he did from his elevated position was to wave with a weak hand, as if he were showering blessings on the hordes. And that, for them, was enough.

He was now in his mid-sixties, and firmly established among all the desert peoples as the one true God's last prophet, the final Messenger, the one true source through which the Creator's will is to be known.

The Messenger had also taken to going on caravan rides. He took with him a company of infantry and two platoons of horsemen. He sat cushioned in a carriage hoisted upon the backs of slaves, Nubians, who had been castrated. In spite of his military accompaniment, his trips were trips of leisure. They were not consistent, but frequent enough and ostentatious enough to be recognized and acknowledged by the ordinary. They bowed, and knelt and cupped their hands and bent their heads to touch the ground in worship. In the shade and comfort of his carriage, he beheld them.

Every now and then, upon a whim, he would stop at the home of his wealthiest followers. He was always showered with gifts of gold, hurriedly prepared meals, and women if needed. On one such whimsical stop, he hobbled into the house of one of his wealthiest followers. The man of the house was away on business, and it fell upon his wife to make appropriate arrangements while servants hurried off to fetch the husband. The family had always dreamed of this blessing, maybe even fantasized about it.

It was a beautiful home, spacious, marble floors hewn smooth, tall ceilings, walls with holy sayings from the mouth of the Messenger printed in the holy language upon the walls. The wife, all aflutter at the appearance of the prophet of the one true God, beckoned her many servants to make appropriate preparations suitable for one whose station was above that of sultans and kings, one who was closest to the Creator of all things.

As if he already knew the place well, the Messenger hobbled directly to the orchard. It was refreshingly shaded by olive trees and dwarf cedars. The woman of the house followed in the wake of the prophet, as would a servant to a master for she had submitted completely. For the children's entertainment, there were swings hung upon the trees in the orchard. The prophet sat upon a swing, shaded, comfortable.

A little girl of five ran up to her mother and clutched her mother's legs as children are wont to do. The mother patted the child's head and bade her thus:

"Go, go to the prophet, the Messenger of God Himself. Go, child."

Hesitantly, the child walked towards the Messenger. He hoisted her upon his lap, touching her pretty little face, holding her arms, hugging her close. The child awakened some almost- -forgotten desire in him. He spoke:

"I will marry this girl. Let your husband make preparations for the wedding in seven days."

"Of course, O Great One! You have honored us and our home. We will make all preparations," she stammered, tears of joy and gratitude running down her cheeks. Without another word, the Messenger took his leave.

The heavily guarded caravan of prophet and soldiers headed back to the military base. They made another stop at an equally well-appointed house. He thought of the child of five. She would need someone mature to help raise her to early girlhood, teach her the ways of submission as he had prescribed in the Holy Book, to care for her physical needs, and teach her the correct ways to serve him, the last and greatest of all prophets to have been sent by the Almighty, the all-seeing, the all-knowing. He could trust none of his other wives to carry out this task, so it must fall upon this new wife.

In that house, he was greeted as expected, with reverence. He insisted on meeting every female in the home who was neither slave nor servant. He chose the sister of the wife of the home. She was pretty enough, mature enough, voluptuous, educated, submissive. She will be well suited to meet his needs and serve as nanny to the child as well until the baby was ready to be truly blessed by him.

He told the mother and father of this home that the wedding will take place at the child's home, but they must take twelve camels for slaughter. There will be two weddings at once. He and his soldiers feasted and left, the image of the child dancing in his mind.

And so it came to pass that on one day the Messenger of the One True God blessed yet another woman and a child by marrying both at once. It was done with much flourish and festivity, as was befitting the last prophet. After the weddings, they headed back to base. A separate tent was erected to accommodate the two new brides, one about thirty-five, the other five.

The adult new bride was subjected to the same treatment as all the others from Kay onwards, save for the third wife who had died in child-birth along with the child she was carrying. There was the quick violation, the kicks, the beatings. The aged man had not changed with time. She was also instructed on the manner in which she should raise the child-bride. She was to dress her as required, with no part exposed to view; she was to learn to be neat and tidy; she was to learn the ways of the new religion; and she was to learn how to revere the messenger himself. She must always submit to the will of the prophet. Always.

The last Messenger took it upon himself to teach her to read and write as he had been taught by Kay. He told her the same stories, with strategic adjustments that inserted himself into all stories and histories. He told her repeatedly of the manner in which the Holy Book was revealed to him by the one true God. He stressed the importance of submission and unquestioning obedience to the one true God through the words of His prophet. The disobedient and the infidel are doomed to hell-fire for all eternity. The child was quick, receptive, frightened.

The Messenger told her that she will be as his daughter until she was older, then she would be his wife, his last wife. This was to be her honor.

Importantly, what she learned from him must not be told to anyone.

Meanwhile, the armies continued to grow in numbers, the many wives continued to be treated in the usual manner, work on the book on the messenger's life and teachings continued, the Messenger's almost magical appearances continued, except now he was accompanied on the platform by the girl-child, covered from head to foot with a transparent cloth over her eyes that she may see without being seen. His army of men thirsty for conquest of lands rich with money and women were placed even farther away so they were but a cheering backdrop to the child and her husband, the holy prophet. All was well.

By the time the child was nine and the messenger nearly seventy, he decided to make her his wife. She was nine. For weeks afterwards, the child sat in corners in shock, her knees raised up to her chin, arms folded tightly around her lower legs. Ever so slowly she found her voice and regained her ability to walk.

The messenger took her everywhere he went, and she was now always in his sumptuous tent. On one journey, the girl needed to relieve herself. The messenger had the caravan stop. He ordered an infantryman go with her and stand guard a discrete distance away from her as she relieved herself behind a dune. The young man did as commanded. The procession continued after she returned to the messenger's covered wagon. The young soldier was never seen or heard from again. Like Kay, he simply vanished.

The messenger died a year or so after this final journey. He wasted away in his bed. In his final hours, he knew that his legacy of greed, cruelty, lust, and death will defeat time and live on long after he was gone. He was right. There is no record of when he died, but there were vague whispers that he died in the warm plushness of his soiled bed. The child-bride was neither seen nor heard from ever again.

BIODATA
DAIZAL R. SAMAD

Daizal Samad is a full professor of English Language and Literature at the University of Guyana. He is the winner of three Best Professor Awards for teaching, scholarship, and administration. **In the Beginning** is his second novel, the first being **The Mirror Tells its Tale**. He has also written a collection of poems, **Rivers Whisper Stars** and edited several books. Samad has published hundreds of scholarly articles and short stories internationally, and he has co-written **A Dictionary of Guyanese Words and Expressions** and **Wholeness and Home in West Indian Literature**. He is currently working on a collection of short stories and another novel. Despite his on-going scholarly and artistic work, Professor Samad's priority is to midwife the next generation of scholars and writers in his native land, Guyana.

www.ingramcontent.com/pod-product-compliance
Lightning Source LLC
LaVergne TN
LVHW041846070526
838199LV00045BA/1456